The Color Book

Sophie Benini Pietromarchi

Translated from the original Italian by
Guido Lagomarsino & edited by Gita Wolf

Tara Books

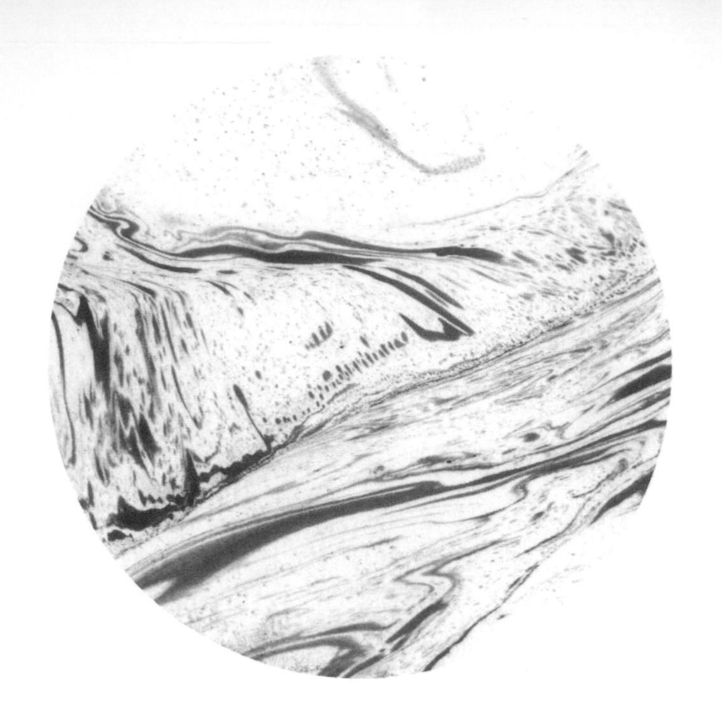

The Color Dance

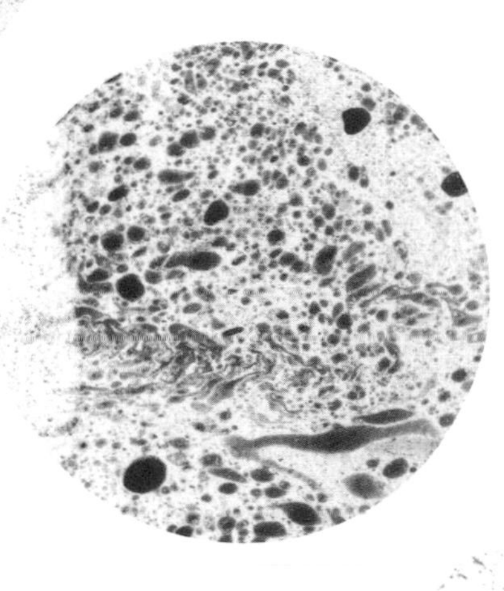

What's my
color book
about?

If you ask me,
I would have preferred to
color quietly, instead
of talking.
I'm marking this great white page
with blue ink, but ideally, I would
rather not have written any words at
all. Color speaks for itself better
than words can – you can "feel"
color, and it goes straight
into your heart.

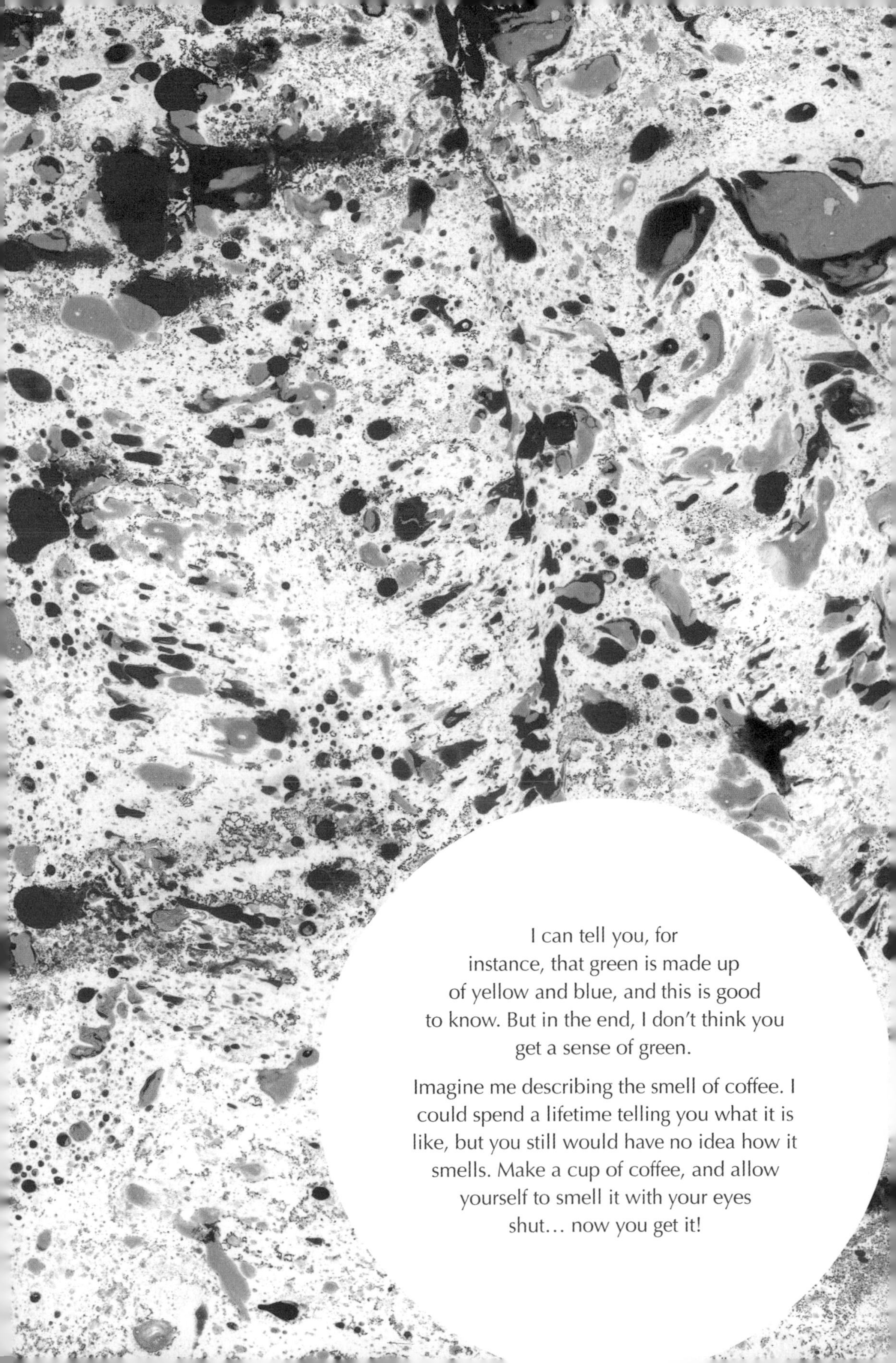

I can tell you, for instance, that green is made up of yellow and blue, and this is good to know. But in the end, I don't think you get a sense of green.

Imagine me describing the smell of coffee. I could spend a lifetime telling you what it is like, but you still would have no idea how it smells. Make a cup of coffee, and allow yourself to smell it with your eyes shut… now you get it!

So what I'm hoping to do
here is to let you actually get to
know colors.
Meet them face to face, by yourself. Not
just through words, but by playing around
them. That's the only way to become friends.

My words are going to take you on a kind of
dance around color – I've even made up a
word for this dance, I'm calling it THE
COLOR DANCE.

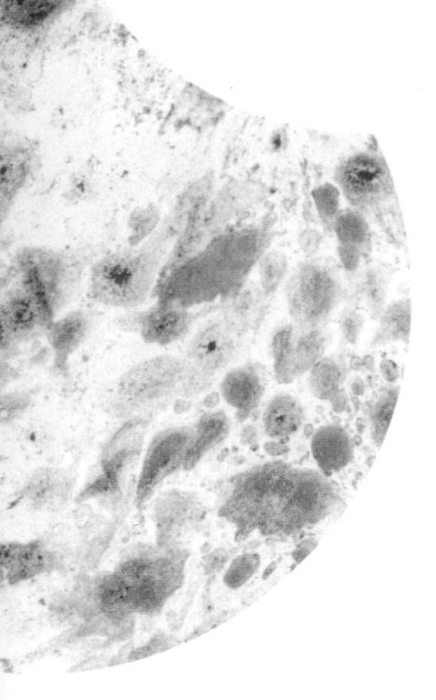

It is a dance
where you don't use
your feet so much as your
eyes, your memory, your
senses and all kinds of other
crazy things… all whirling
around those mysterious
things called
colors.

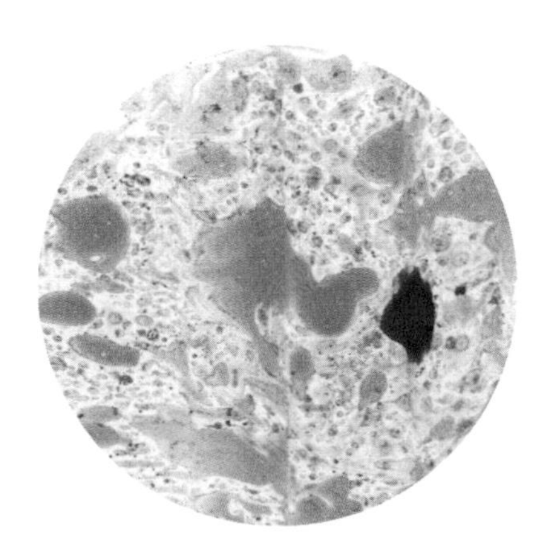

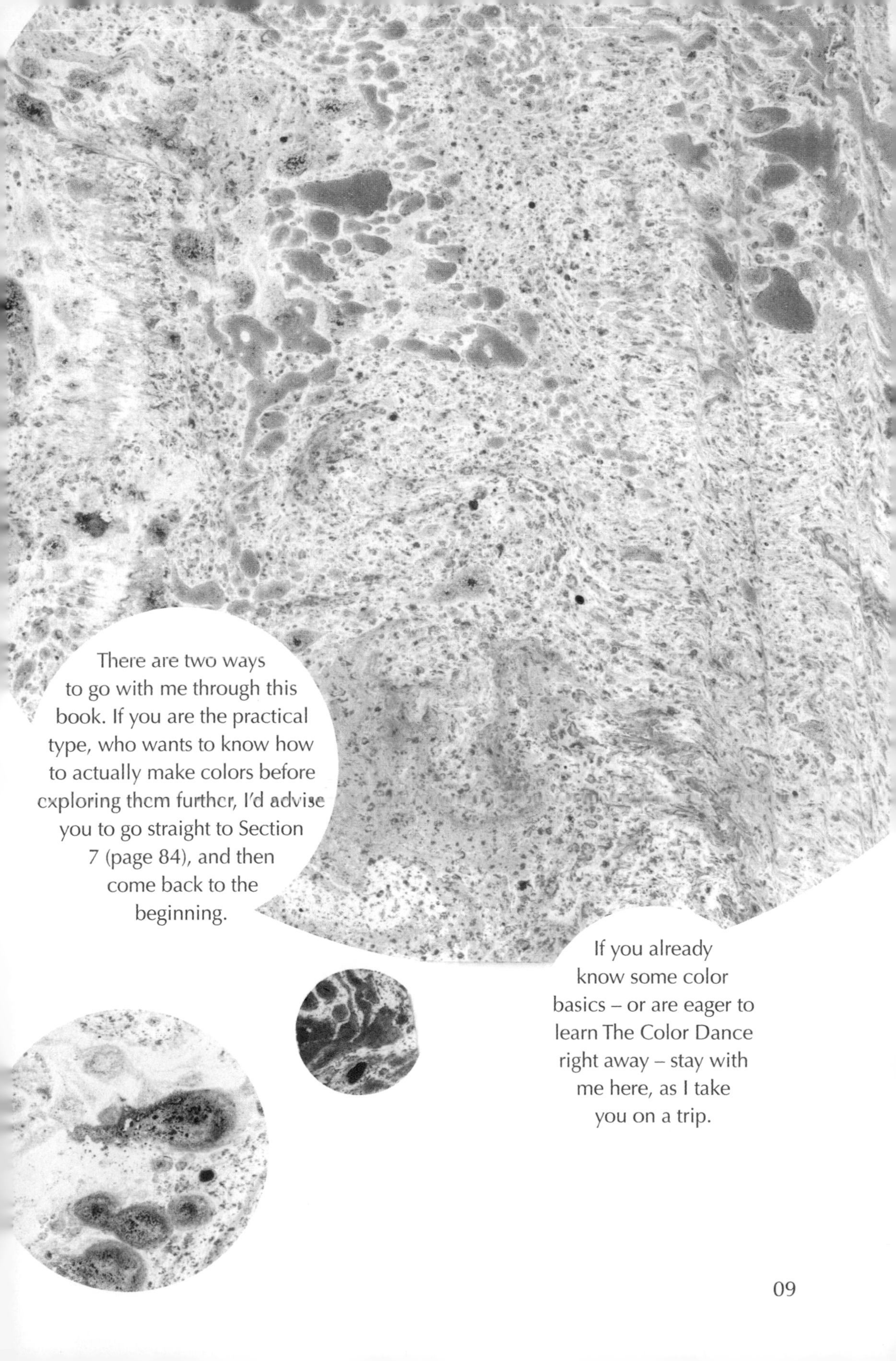

There are two ways to go with me through this book. If you are the practical type, who wants to know how to actually make colors before exploring them further, I'd advise you to go straight to Section 7 (page 84), and then come back to the beginning.

If you already know some color basics – or are eager to learn The Color Dance right away – stay with me here, as I take you on a trip.

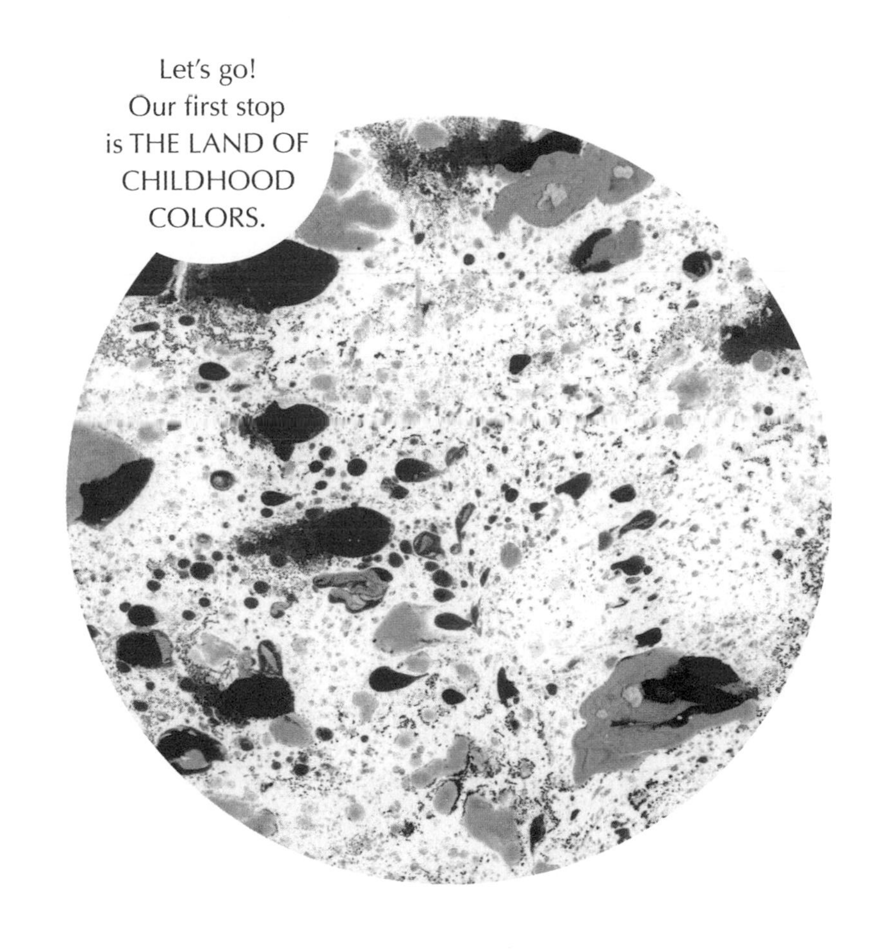
Let's go!
Our first stop
is THE LAND OF
CHILDHOOD
COLORS.

1 The Land of Childhood

Colors

1.1 Remembering Feelings

Let me tell you what I remember from my own land of childhood colors.

As a child, when I lived in a small village in Spain, I always walked barefoot. The ground was dusty, and when I walked, my feet picked up the fine dust. They were coated with a dull layer of film, the color of fog, like the feet of a plaster statue. Then I would wash my feet in a fountain, and they changed back again into the glistening, brilliant color of wet skin.

— I learned later that when you apply a thin layer of white on colors that are dry, it behaves like this fine dust, creating a dull surface that subdues the original color.

My mother is a sculptor. Once, when she was modeling my head in clay, I tried to run away from the room. She chuckled, and held me back with her clayey dark gray hands. When her fingers dried, they turned a light gray.

— *Some colors turn lighter when they dry.*

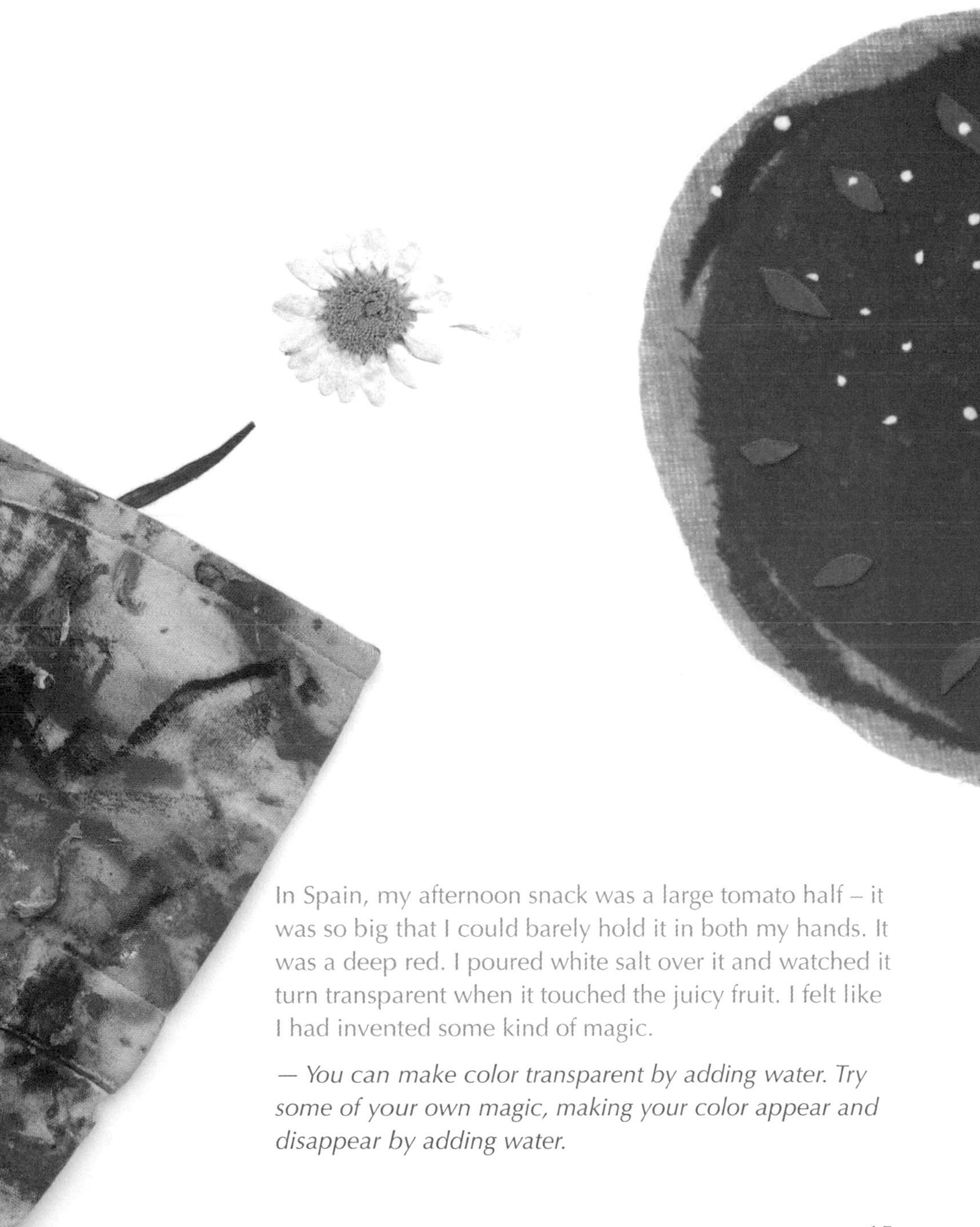

In Spain, my afternoon snack was a large tomato half – it was so big that I could barely hold it in both my hands. It was a deep red. I poured white salt over it and watched it turn transparent when it touched the juicy fruit. I felt like I had invented some kind of magic.

— *You can make color transparent by adding water. Try some of your own magic, making your color appear and disappear by adding water.*

I'm trying to think of a green memory. It would be the lawn where my father would lie with his arms wide open, and then fall asleep in the afternoon.

— Green, for me, is my father's warm sense of peace on a sunny afternoon.

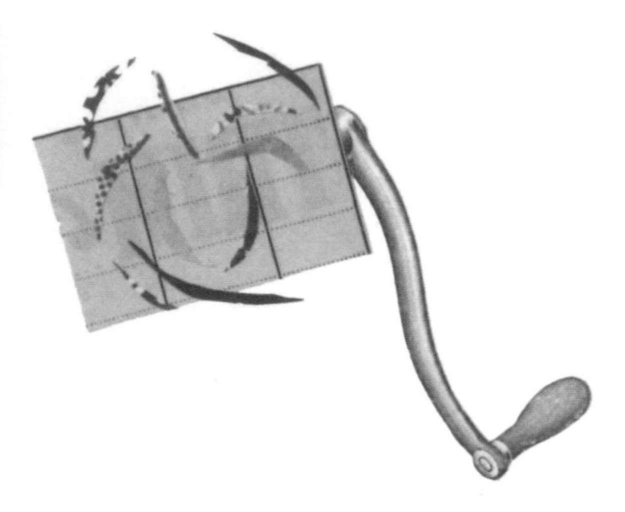

I remember a toy my brother and I used to play with: it was an open box where you could pin a white postcard. There was a small motor that you turned on to make the card spin. We would pour a few drops of color on the whirling card – yellow, blue, red, purple, green – then carefully turn off the motor. It was amazing! The most beautiful images would appear.

— I think this is where I learned to use color fearlessly. But I also learned to stop in time, because if I poured in too much color, the whole thing turned into a real mess.

I can't help connecting the color black with the deafening noise of coal chucked into an oven at night. My father would wake up in the middle of the night to fill the stove, and the shower of coal nuggets would regularly wake us up from our dreams.

— So color was connected to hearing, I realized, but it can be linked to other senses too: sight, smell, touch and taste.

Pink makes me remember the candies I bought after school, they turned my tongue pink.

— When I see something pink, it brings back the sweet taste of that color.

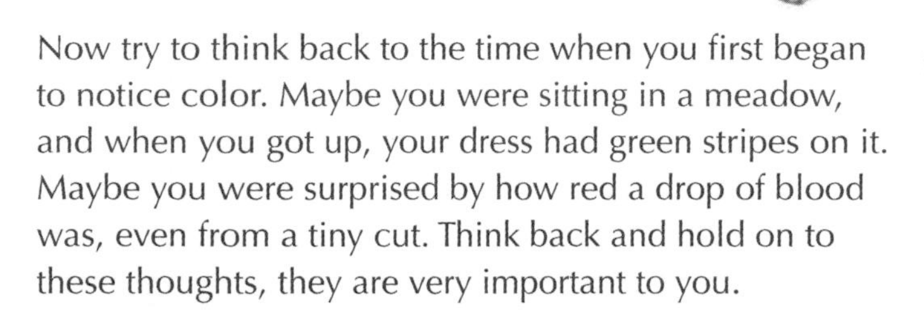

Now try to think back to the time when you first began to notice color. Maybe you were sitting in a meadow, and when you got up, your dress had green stripes on it. Maybe you were surprised by how red a drop of blood was, even from a tiny cut. Think back and hold on to these thoughts, they are very important to you.

1.2 Mixing It All Up

Have you ever tried to cover a stick with mud? How about pouring juice on a plate? As you were doing these things, did you notice how the color changed? You probably had to go about it very carefully… we all love to mix things, to create magic potions.

Each of us has our own special ingredients – earth, nettles, pebbles, flowers, mud… and we know

Mixing
a color is like
creating a
magic potion.
Each ingredient
has its own
special power and
way of behaving.
The way they are
put together creates
a new color, with its
own special personality.
You might, for instance,
use a green nettle leaf
when you want to make a
magical poisonous potion.
Or you might go for a muddy
yellow.

Try to think of colors as characters with their own personalities. Now let's invent a few and see what kind of powers they have.

2 A Word Dance

Starring Color Characters

I started out by telling you that I didn't want to speak much. But there is something I need to show you, and for that I need to use words, lots of them. It's part of my Color Dance. I'm now going to dance around with words – and with some characters I made up. Who are they and how many types of them are there? They're colors!

You don't need to do much, just be swept along with me, allow my words to play a while in your mind, and you'll be surprised by what happens.

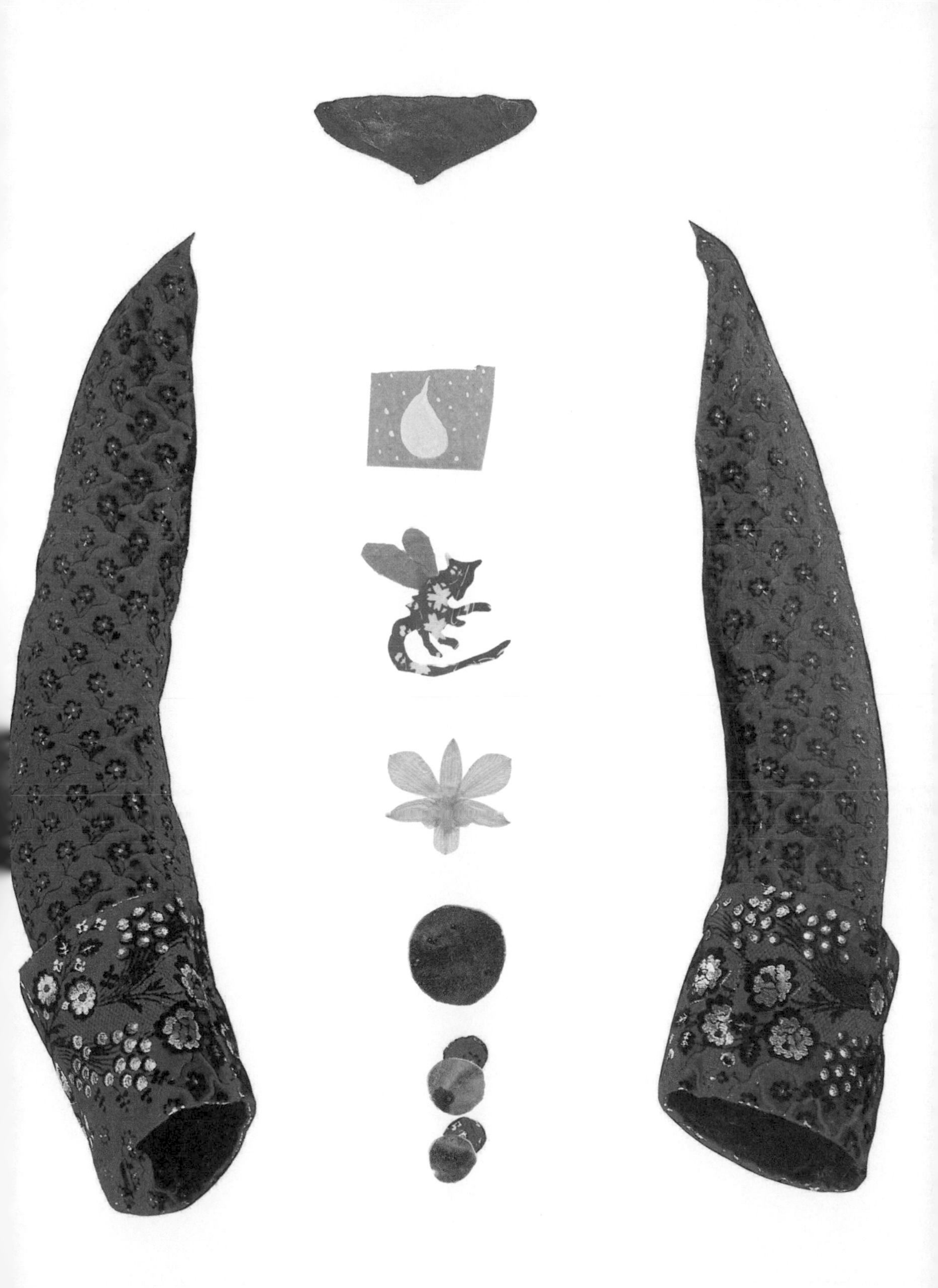

2.1 The Red Dragon

RED IS A DRAGON with hot blood, which is warm and red, warming next to a fire. He can be affectionate, but he also relishes violence and bloodshed. He eats pomegranates, strawberries, and – yes – tomatoes! On certain nights, when the moon is red, he wears a magnificent crimson robe, the envy of kings. He spits fire with great dignity, breathing out fierce glowing golden embers, quite unaware of how ferocious he is. Despite his accessories, he's never met Santa Claus. But he did let Red Riding Hood try his winged crown. The dragon loves red pepper sweets. In the afternoon he takes a siesta in a poppy field and when he wakes up, watches a blazing sunset in the evening, his wings drooping with awe.

When he goes into town, he often stands in a daze in front of traffic lights. You've got to understand our dragon – yes, he's rash, but he certainly knows where not to go, it's like he has a sign in his mind saying – STOP!

Now that you know the character of the dragon a little, you will realize that dabbing on a spot of red is like inviting the hot dragon in. So yellow on a red dragon becomes a warm orange. Blue changes the dragon's aggression into a more peaceful violet. White sweetens him into a lovely pink. If a little bit of the dragon touches black, it changes from dark to brown – the color of earth.

2,2 The Yellow Bird of Paradise

YELLOW IS A BIRD OF PARADISE – wearing a flowery scent. Her eyes are two glowing lanterns, and she lives in a castle of straw with a thousand rooms. She dusts her hair with pollen. Her bed is made of sunflowers, and her pillows of bananas and lemons. She loves to peck on cobs of corn. She flies on rays of light, and sometimes, when she is close to the sun, her voice turns golden. She can strike precisely, like a flash of lightning, or glow with a mellow light as the seasons change.

When you add a small feather of the yellow bird into another color, you bring in a glowing secret. Green turns bright: fresh and new, like tiny blossoming leaves. A bit of yellow in pink raises it to an elegant salmon. A yellow feather tossed into blue makes turquoise, the color of peacocks. Yellow in black is unexpected, heavy but interesting.

2.3 The Great Blue Feather

THE GREAT BLUE FEATHER is in fact many-colored, as it floats through the night, far out into the heavens. It lies in wait for that exact instant when a line appears between sea and sky, and morning is born. It then flies through the blue sky, dodging white clouds, crossing oceans, rivers and ponds, picking up glints of North Pole ice, landing finally into a water glass, giving it a sharp cold stir. It can be cheerful and summery, but is also very moody, becoming deep and sad in shadowy rooms.

A blue feather cools other colors, but also gives them a serious, deep touch, like a vast starlit sky. Yellow becomes complex, red calms down into a mysterious purple, orange goes out like a fire. A dab of blue turns white heavenly, but black angry and shiny.

2.4 The White Angel

THE WHITE ANGEL drinks vanilla milk from frosted glasses, mixing it with sugar and salt. She loves smiley music, but she can also turn pale with fear. She drifts over clouds, trailing a snowy soft veil that covers the earth with a carpet of flour. She lives in a fog, in the misty light of early morning when imaginary castles disappear. She knows the Milky Way, the hair of wise men and the white of the eye. She embroiders candy floss threads. She is pure and open, casting light wherever she goes.

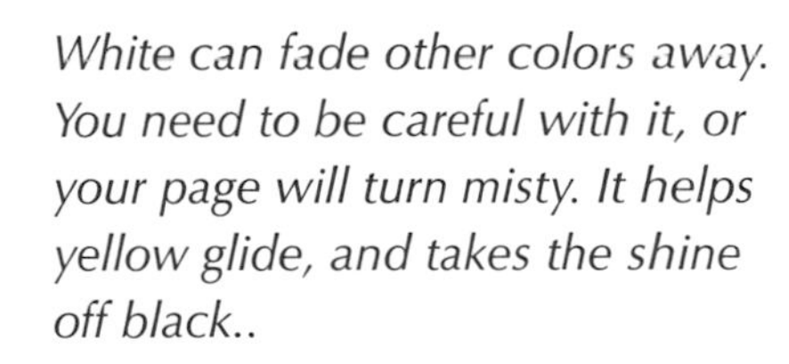

White can fade other colors away. You need to be careful with it, or your page will turn misty. It helps yellow glide, and takes the shine off black..

2.5 The Black Lion

The BLACK LION is strong and elegant. He roars in a dark storm, and when he yawns, you can see the stars in his maw. He loves caves, vases and the depths of the sea. When he is in a black mood, he covers himself with crow feathers and waves a fan of beetle wings. When he calms down, he moves beautifully along inky trails, and his lines turn into writing. The mane of the Black Lion is made up of all the shadows in the world, and when his tail swishes, he conjures up new ones.

Black frightens every other color
when he passes by, roaring and
scratching the paper.
No one dares to reply.
Mauve wouldn't
exist without
him.

2.6 The Brown Snail

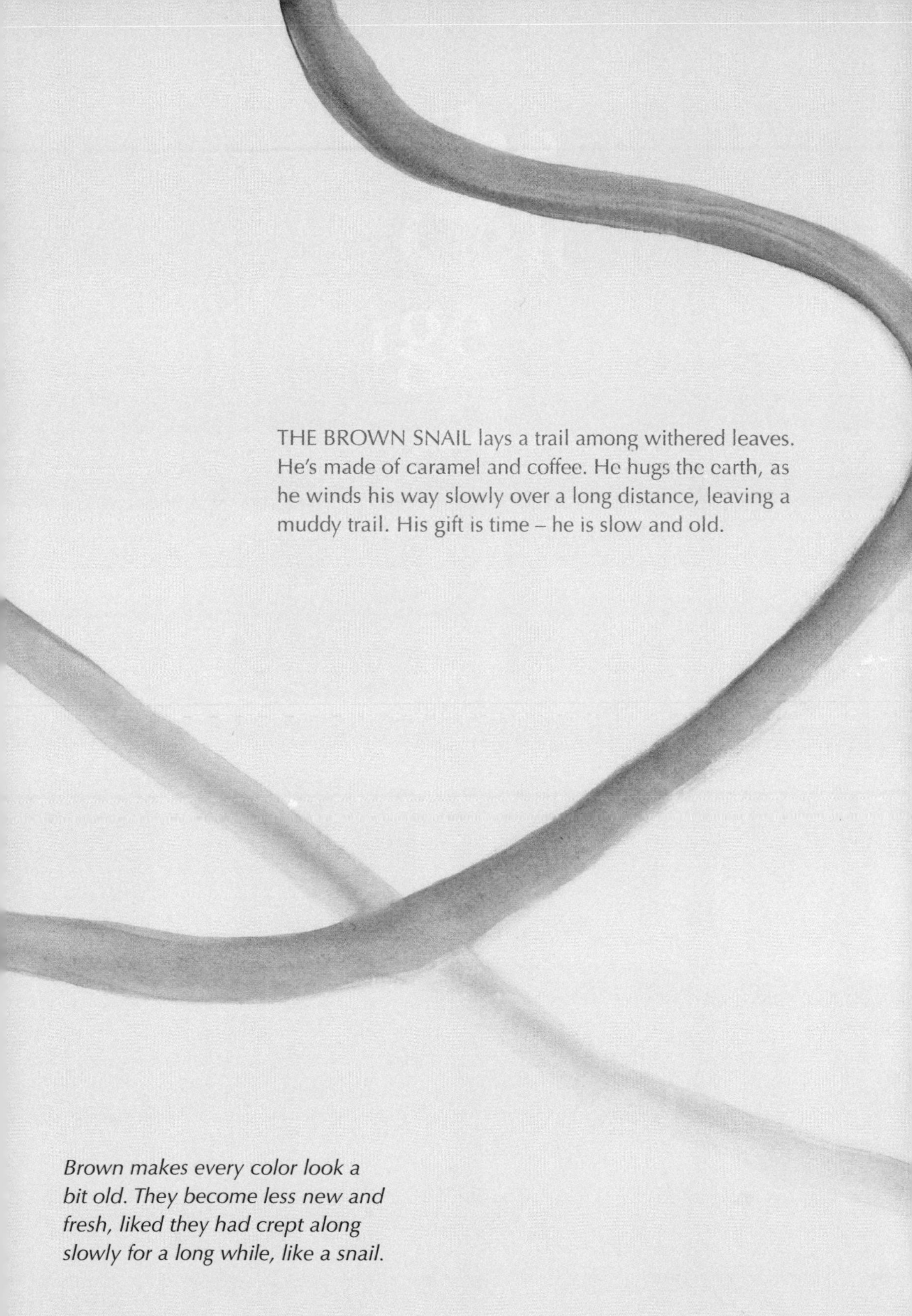

THE BROWN SNAIL lays a trail among withered leaves. He's made of caramel and coffee. He hugs the earth, as he winds his way slowly over a long distance, leaving a muddy trail. His gift is time – he is slow and old.

Brown makes every color look a bit old. They become less new and fresh, liked they had crept along slowly for a long while, like a snail.

3 The Color Cage

Now that you've entered the world of color, let's turn your attention to your paintbox.

Hmmm... don't colors in a box seem like birds shut up in a cage? The poor creatures don't know where to go, they know nothing outside their cage. So let's free them, and see where they go.

3.1 The Dance of the Glance

How can you free colors from being locked up?
By using your eyes. Look… LOOK… LOOK AROUND! Look out of the box! Don't be afraid, let your glance dance around the place.

This is part of the Color Dance.

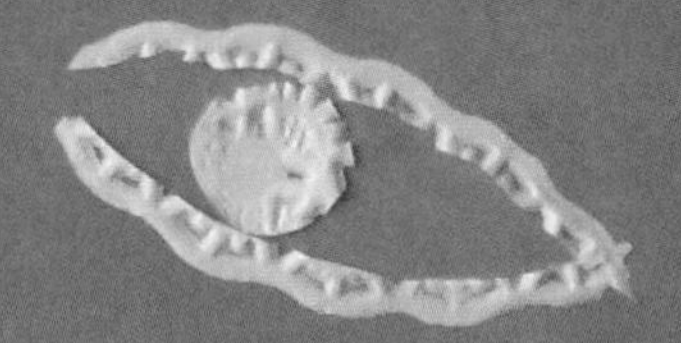

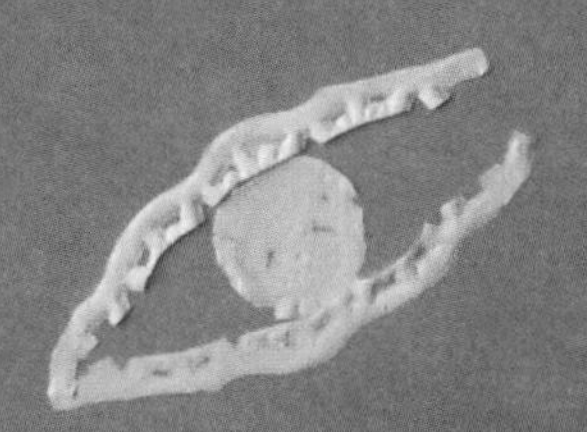

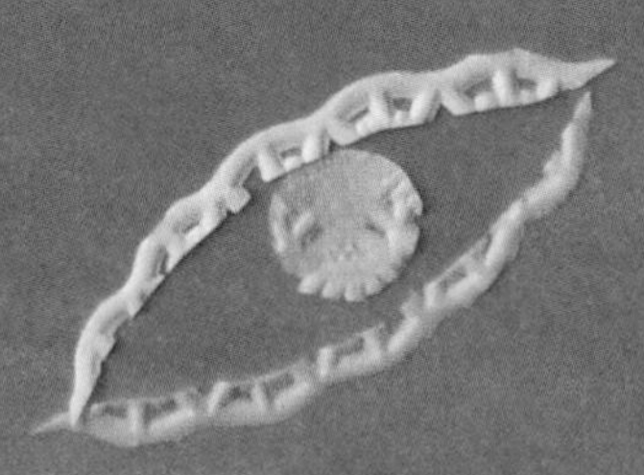

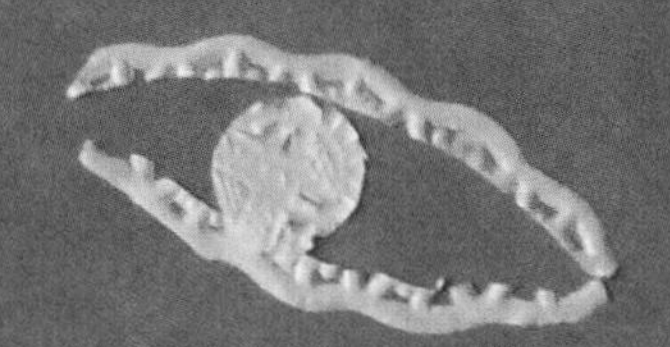

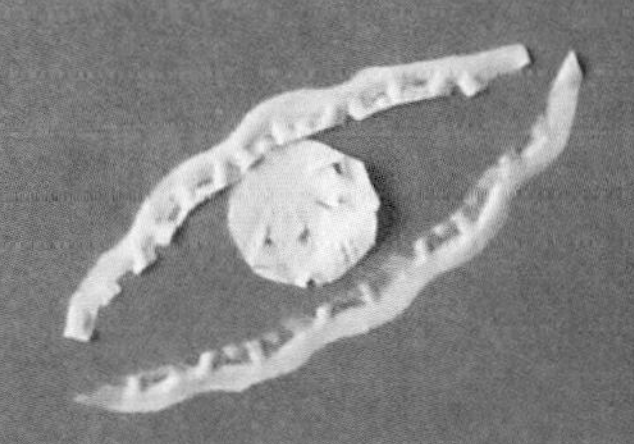

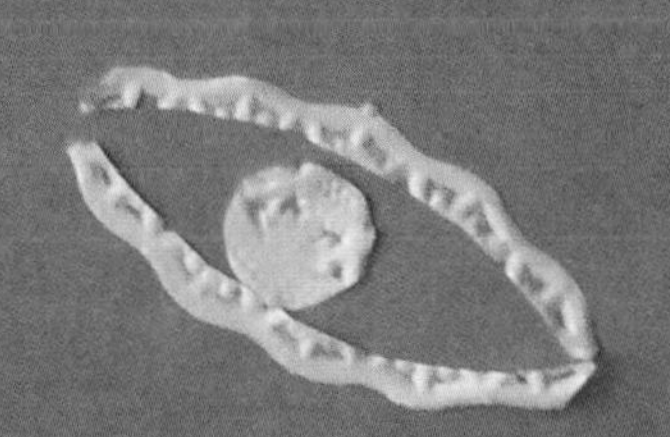

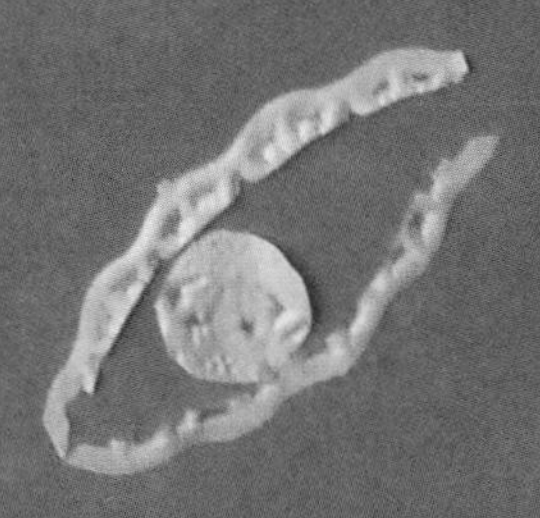

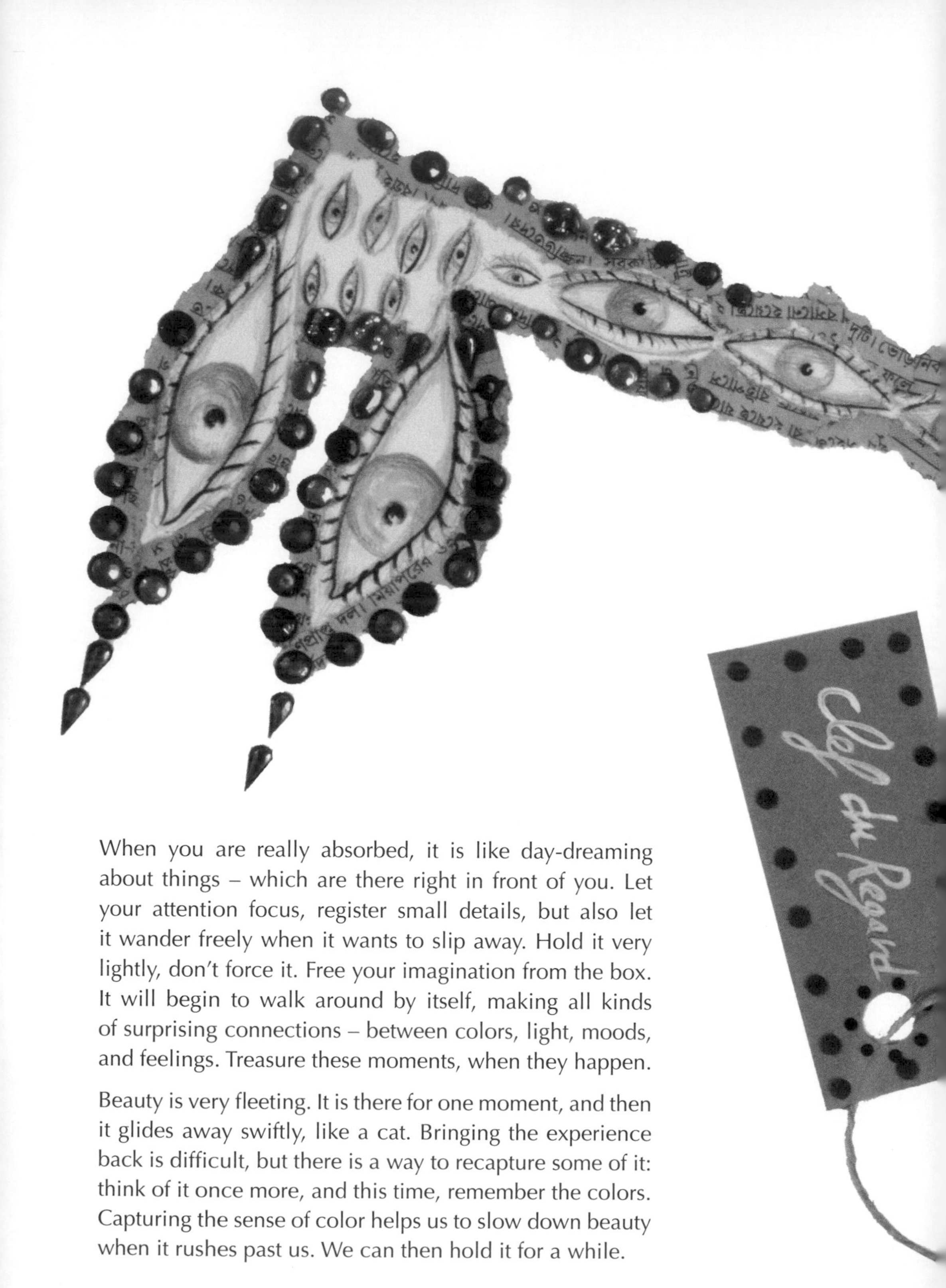

When you are really absorbed, it is like day-dreaming about things – which are there right in front of you. Let your attention focus, register small details, but also let it wander freely when it wants to slip away. Hold it very lightly, don't force it. Free your imagination from the box. It will begin to walk around by itself, making all kinds of surprising connections – between colors, light, moods, and feelings. Treasure these moments, when they happen.

Beauty is very fleeting. It is there for one moment, and then it glides away swiftly, like a cat. Bringing the experience back is difficult, but there is a way to recapture some of it: think of it once more, and this time, remember the colors. Capturing the sense of color helps us to slow down beauty when it rushes past us. We can then hold it for a while.

So you need to learn to look twice. The first time with amazement, and the second time by remembering the colors. That's the key I'm giving you now: it is the double-take, the glance that looks twice. It's like going to a place two times. Let's go.

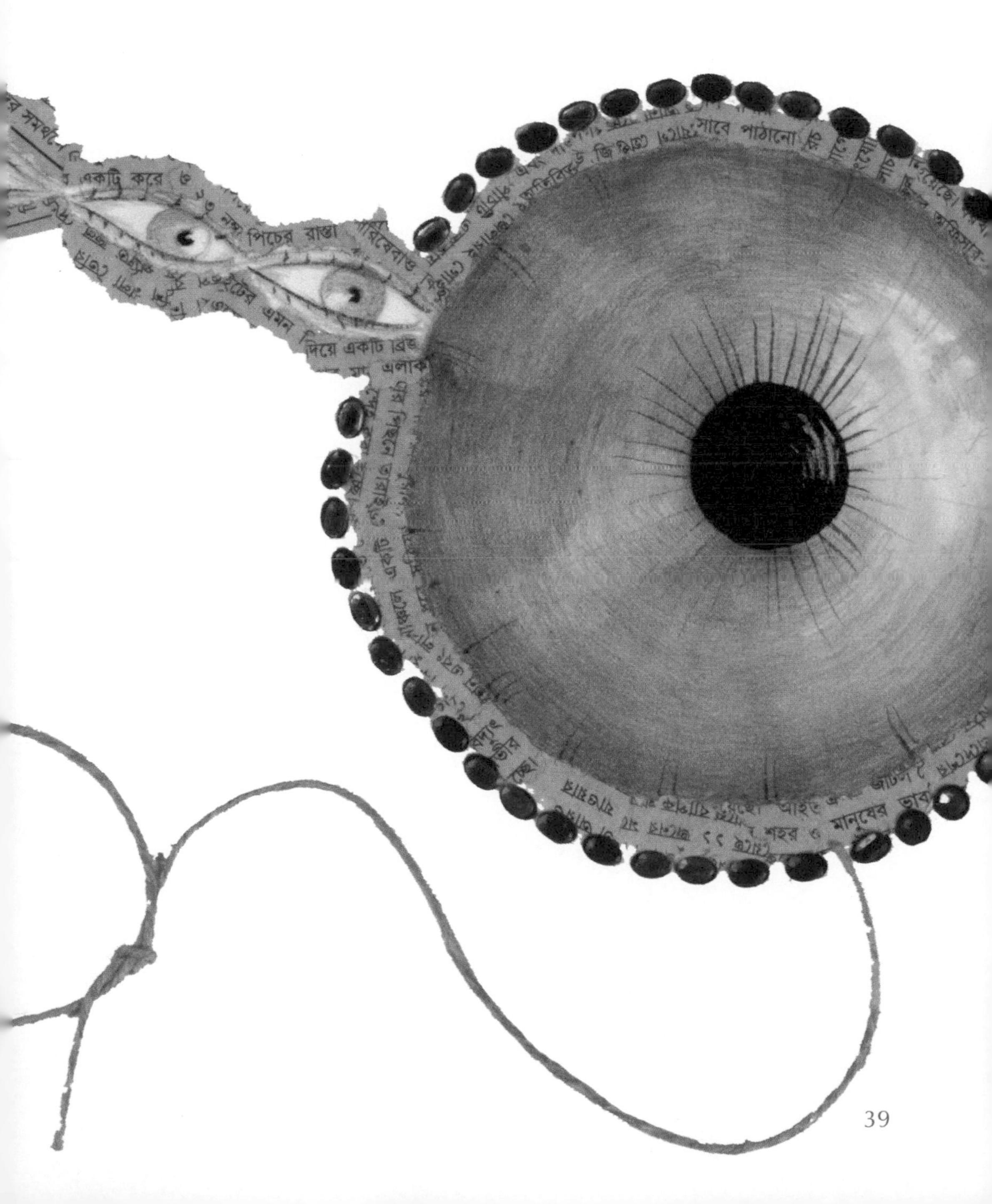

3.2 The Forest of Color

Color is everywhere, but also in us, in our minds.

Say you go on a treasure hunt, and collect an assortment of little objects. Now sort them out into color groups on a board – you can't be too strict, and you can't be too lenient, just be playfully systematic – and soon you'll realize that you're making sense of the swarm of color that surrounds you. This system doesn't have a beginning or an end, it is just an order – your order.

When you do this, you'll notice that you wander from one object to the other peacefully, without thinking too much. And then, if you turn your eyes away and come back to the board, you might realize that you've made something precious for yourself: it's a little shrine of color, a place where you can spend time looking around and musing, a place of what we could call contemplation. It's your own forest of color.

Do you want to look into my shrine?

BROWN

WHITE

YELLOW
mel

ORANGE
Hollywood

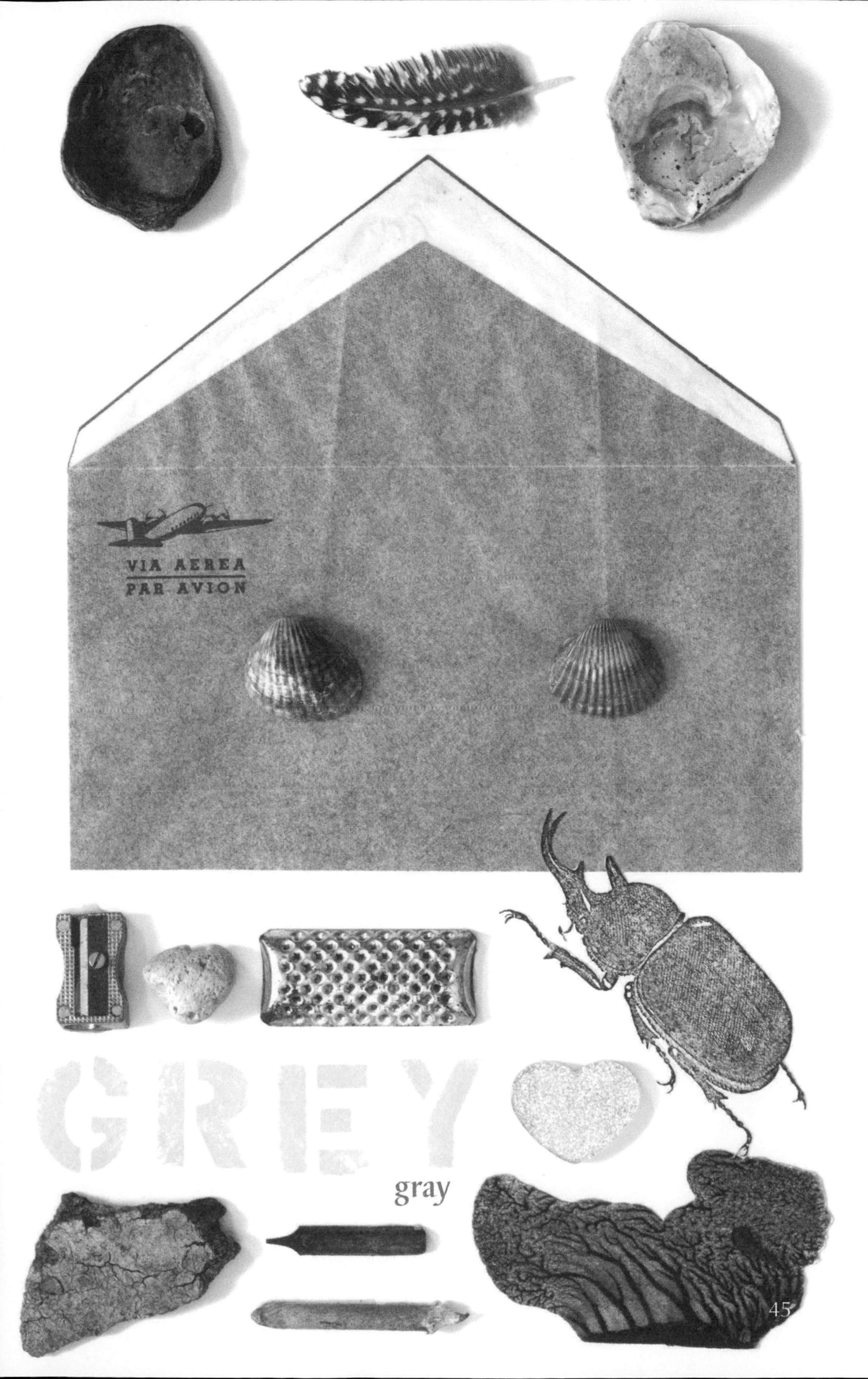
VIA AEREA
PAR AVION
GREY
gray

BLACK
FEDERICO FELLINI
ITALIA
€ 0,60

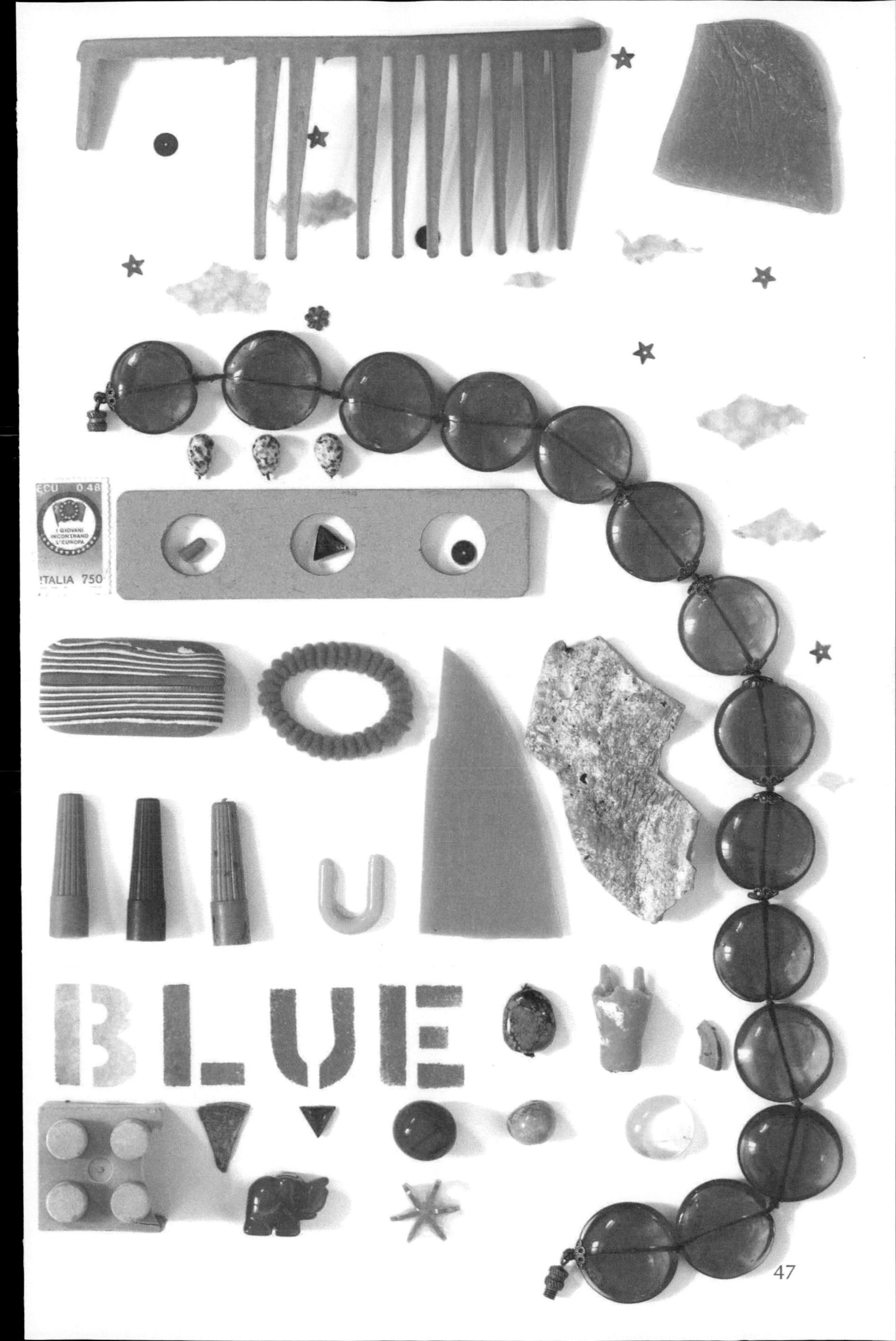
ECU 0.48
I GIOVANI INCONTRANO L'EUROPA
ITALIA 750
BLUE

CAMPARI SODA
LOVE
2·3·4·5
premio
RED

VIOLET
SUPREME
Ravalgaon

PINK
AMOUR

FRANCE
1,10
FRANCE
1,10
GREEN

4 Nature

4.1 Picture Explorer

Another way of collecting colors is through images – through photographs and drawings. You can create these yourself, or collect pictures made by others.

They could be part of your surroundings,
they could be in nature, or in the city

It's great to wander around, notice a detail,
take a photo, or note quickly in a notebook…

For a color explorer, everything – even the most boring wall or a small yellow door – is interesting.

Color is in everything – in the feathers of a bird, in a dream, in a film… it can even come up in a vague feeling.

You begin to think of meanings and making connections. When you do that, color lets you travel, across all these realms.

4.2 Turning Nature Upside-down

Nature is bursting with color… this is nothing new to most of us, so I thought I'd look at it another way.

I want to turn things upside down, and think about impossible colors, which we would never find in nature. So my Color Dance here will show you that "wrong" colors can have all sorts of effects: they can make an image weaker… or, strangely, better and stronger. Here are some impossible colors, see what you make of them.

The Pink Wolf is still impressive, but he's lost his ferociousness and I doubt whether he'd freeze the blood of anyone who meets him.

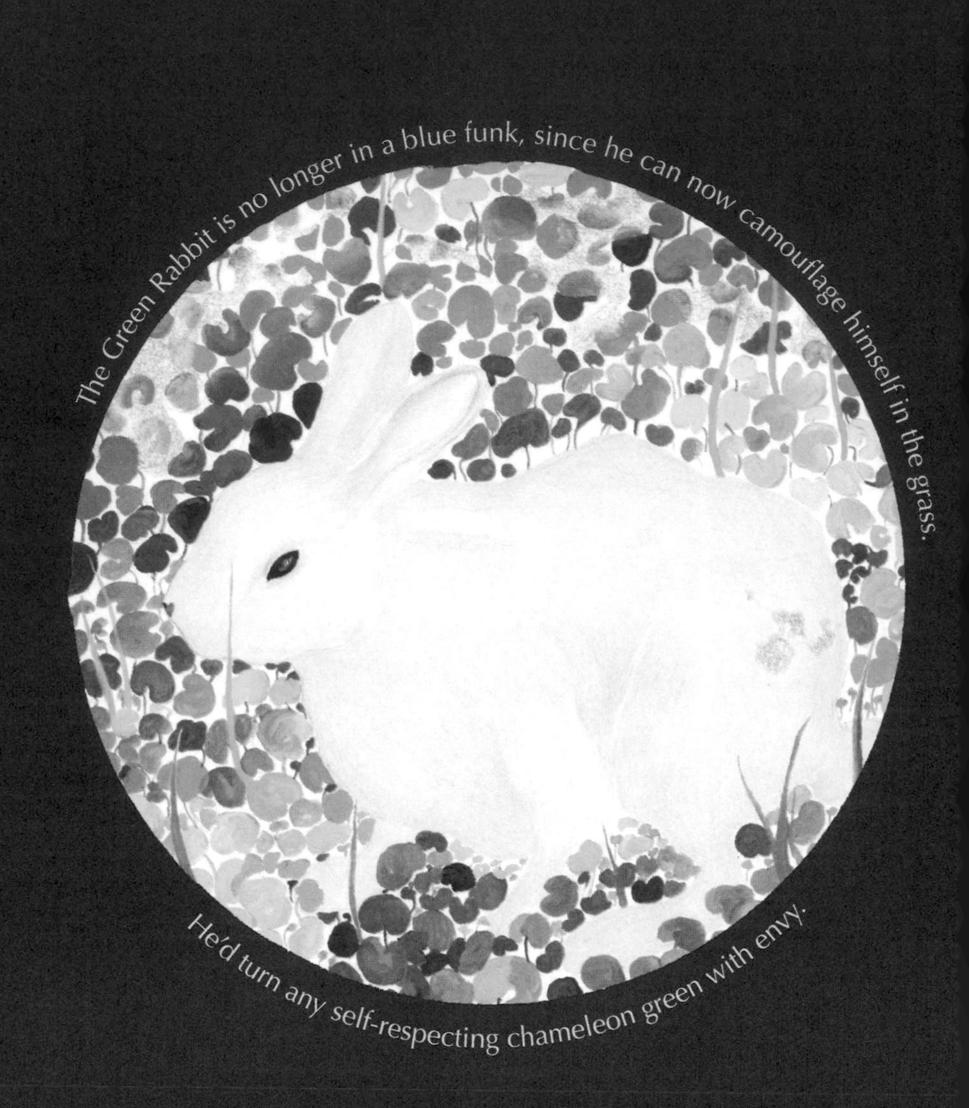

The Green Rabbit is no longer in a blue funk, since he can now camouflage himself in the grass.

He'd turn any self-respecting chameleon green with envy.

And the Orange Rhino? I'm thinking that he's sweet, and really crazy about marshmallows.

The Blue Chihuahua looks like snow melting in the spring.

Listen to that wagging tail, it sounds like an ice-cream bell!

The Red-and-White Striped Zebra? I'm wondering what kind of character he'd have.

Any ideas?

The Yellow Elephant collects pollen with his trunk, and sprays it on himself like a cloak. He's a great attraction for the bees.

5 Moods

Colors are associated with moods in different ways. Let's look at some of them.

5.1 Feelings

Now that we've played with "wrong" colors, I think the Color Dance should also help you look at actual colors. The thing to keep in mind is that colors change all the time. Much depends on the time of day, the weather, the seasons: a black sky makes the colors we look at dark and gloomy, while under a clear blue sky, all the colors stand out happily. In a way, this applies to people's mood as well…

Connecting moods with color is something we do instinctively, and even small children have a feel for it. I remember scolding my tiny daughter Matilde once – she was quiet, but after a while, came to me with a sheet of paper with huge black scribbles on it. She'd drawn our fight, using angry little strokes! I had no choice but to relent and make peace.

5.2 Color Faces

We "read" faces all the time – even if a person doesn't say anything, we look at her face, and realize she's angry or sad or happy. We even know when someone says they're happy, but they are actually not.

It works with photographs as well. You can read a lot from portraits, if you look carefully. In this one here, for instance, it would be right to say that her eyes are smiling, even though her mouth is hidden by her hand. Her smile is shy and playful. What kind of person is she? What does the rest of the face say? How old is she, do you think? What is she thinking? What does she like, can you guess?

You could say that my Color Dance is making you ask personal questions. It certainly encourages you to be curious and curiosity is a wonderful quality, especially when you try to read color, in the way you read faces. You can actually learn to do that – look at colors, understand how they are made up, what feelings and moods they can call up. And when you do get to know them like this, you'll be able to use colors in a personal way, and create a world for yourself.

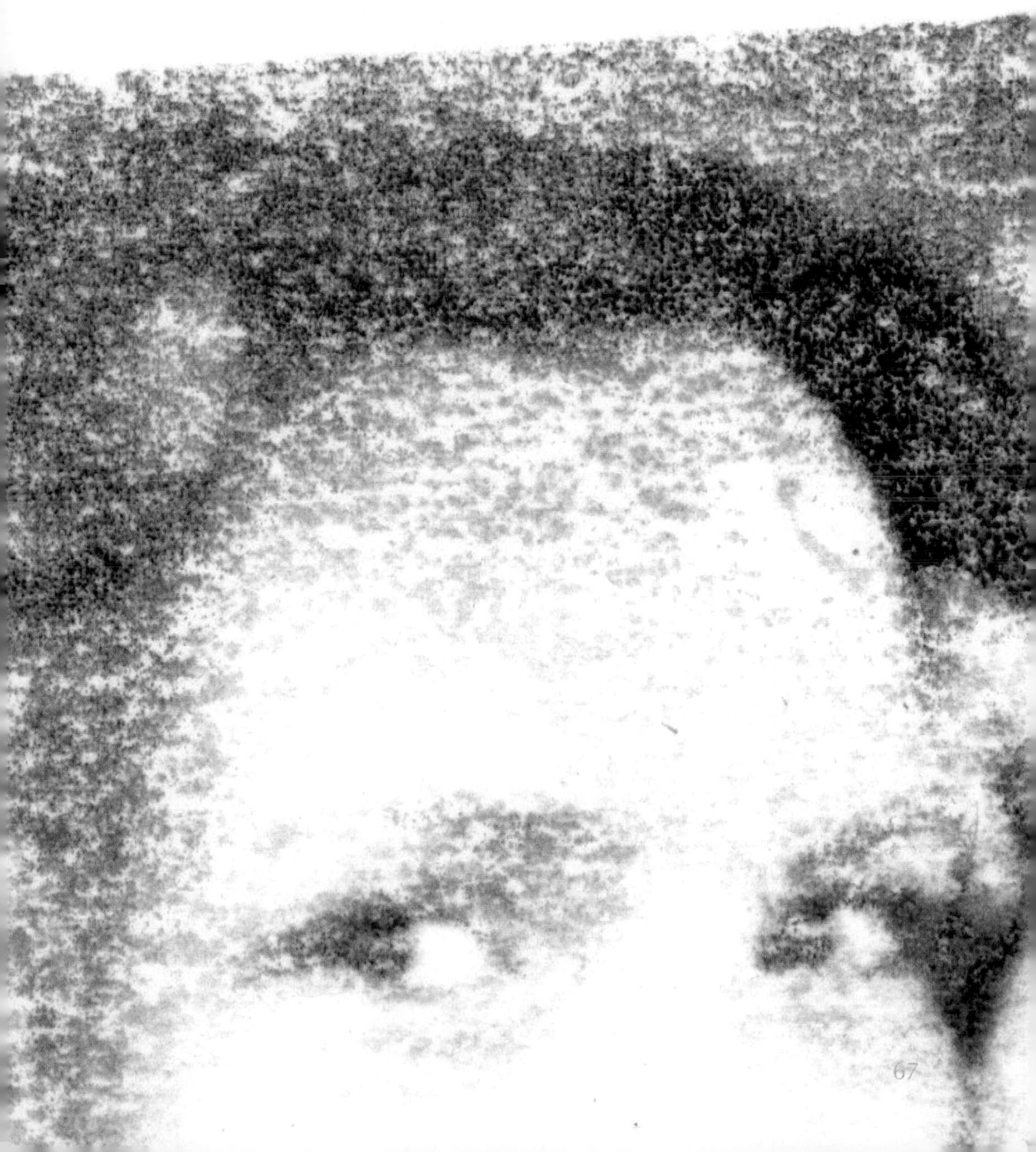

Take this yellow. To me, it is a very full yellow, like it has something darker inside, something almost ancient like an old deep yolk. The edges are lighter and brighter. I think of saffron, of spices, and of India.

I've made up a little quiz to ask the yellow – and what my answers would be, if I was that yellow – which gives you an idea of how to go about this exercise.

What color are you?

Yellow

What shade are you?

You could say I go from a golden yellow to a dark ochre

What other colors are you made of?

I may have a tinge of red, mixed in with an earthy yellow

What do you make people think of?

A broken egg from long ago?

What can I do with you?

You could paint some flowers, or a shadowy yellow house

What kind of color are you painted with?

Tempera, but you can use poster colors or acrylic as well

I'm sure you can think of even more questions to ask. When you do this exercise on your own, don't be afraid to use a lot of words. The more words you use, the richer your understanding.

5.3 Color Feelings

So let's continue matching moods and colors,
in our Color Dance, and see where it takes us.

Here's a shy little girl, she's probably watching an adult, and biting her lower lip nervously.

Shy Colors

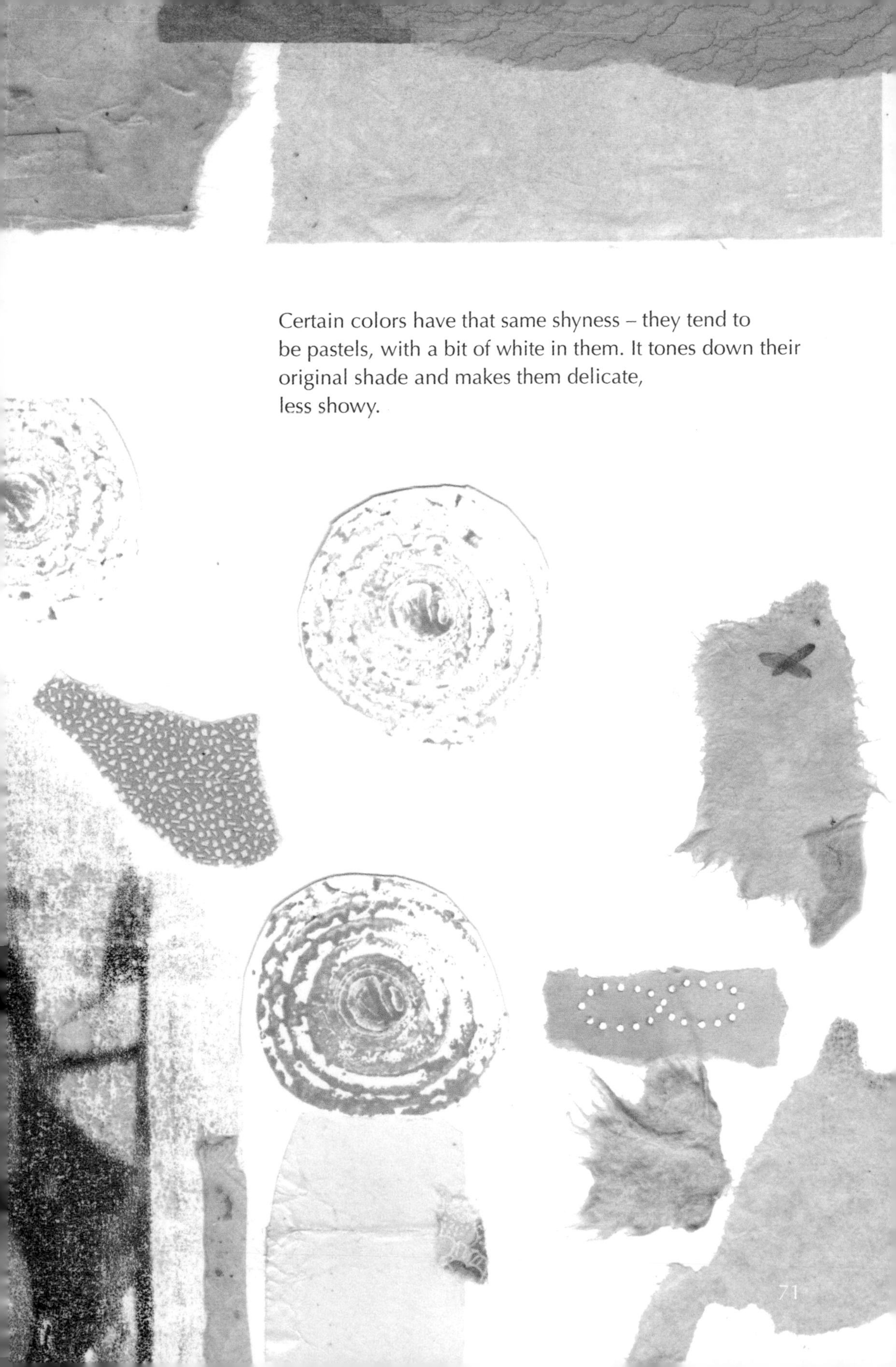

Certain colors have that same shyness – they tend to be pastels, with a bit of white in them. It tones down their original shade and makes them delicate, less showy.

Clashing Colors

This boy is grimacing with disgust, and when you look at the colors, they'll probably make you grimace too. It's not that they are awful in themselves, but they clash together. They seem to be fighting each other, when they're placed side by side. So the effect that colors have on each other is just as important as the colors themselves.

Smiling Colors

Here's a sunny, laughing face. And the surrounding colors are equally happy – cheerful, strong and direct.

6 Color Probes

One way to get to know a whole range of colors is by giving them names. The names are almost like little probes, samplers that you dip in and out of colors, to see what they are like. You can come up with your own names: funny ones, dreamy ones, crazy ones…

6.1 Color Names

Here is a list of names, from my part of the world in Europe. These colors could have very different names in your area. Why don't you find the equivalents? You could also make a list of your local colors.

Aquamarine (pale blue-green)
Prussian Blue (dark blue)
Cornflower Blue (light blue)
Sugar Paper (blue gray)
Blue Ash (light blue-gray-white)
Turtle Dove (beige-pink-gray-black)
Sage (greenish gray)
Pearl Gray (the color of dark beads)
London Fog (gray)
Tea Leaf (from blue to green)
Emerald Green (like a gemstone)
Moss Green (bright green with a bit of gray)
Olive Green (yellowish green)
Aubergine (purple to brown)
Periwinkle (blue-violet-gray)

Robin’s Egg (blue)
Burnt Umber
(very dark brown)
Chocolate (deep brown)
Champagne Yellow
(like a straw yellow
with a sparkle)
Canary Yellow
(a bright yellow)
Lemon Yellow
(an acid yellow)
Asparagus Yellow (a pale yellow)
Sulphur (a soft yellow)
Saffron (a deep vivid yellow)
Mustard (yellow with a bit
of ochre)
Taxi Yellow
Cherry (the color
of the fruit)
Peach Pink (the color of the fruit)
Cardinal Red (color of
a church cardinal's clothes
– a full bright red)
Coral (red with pink-orange)

6.2 Personal Colors

Here's a Color Dance game I've invented, which helps you to mix, invent, and relate in your own special way to colors. You need two baskets – one with a random list of words, and one with names of colors.

You draw two or three words from the word basket and one from the color basket.

Say the color you've picked up is BLUE.

Now the first word you have is DAWN. What kind of blue does dawn suggest? Something soft and light? Paint a patch of this blue.

Your next word is ANGRY. What is an angry blue? Dark? Think about this, and paint it. Now combine the two colors you've painted, by painting one on top of the other, or mixed together. You have now invented a new color: ANGRY DAWN BLUE!

angry

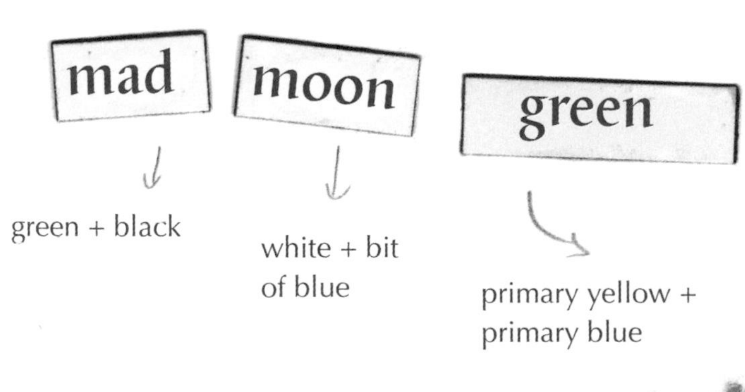

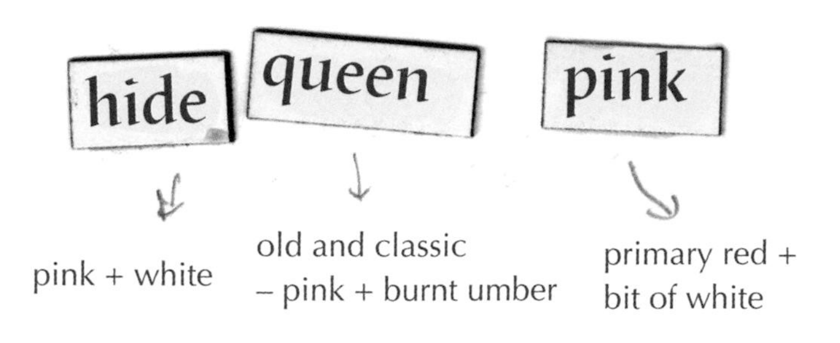

You can make whole books of invented colors, and as you go along, you will get a sense of how layered colors are, and where to look for them. By connecting colors to different kinds of words, you'll see that colors relate not only to seeing, but also to feeling, thinking, touching, smelling and understanding.

Blue can have the smell of salt, just like you hear the sea in a shell. Pink can have the taste of sugar. Red is like touching a hot iron. Green has the rough feel of mown grass. These are my personal connections, and you will have yours. Color can be a very personal experience, because you combine your associations in a way that cannot be explained – it is yours to see, feel, touch, smell and know. The one thing to keep in mind is that colors reflect things around them, and all things reflect color.

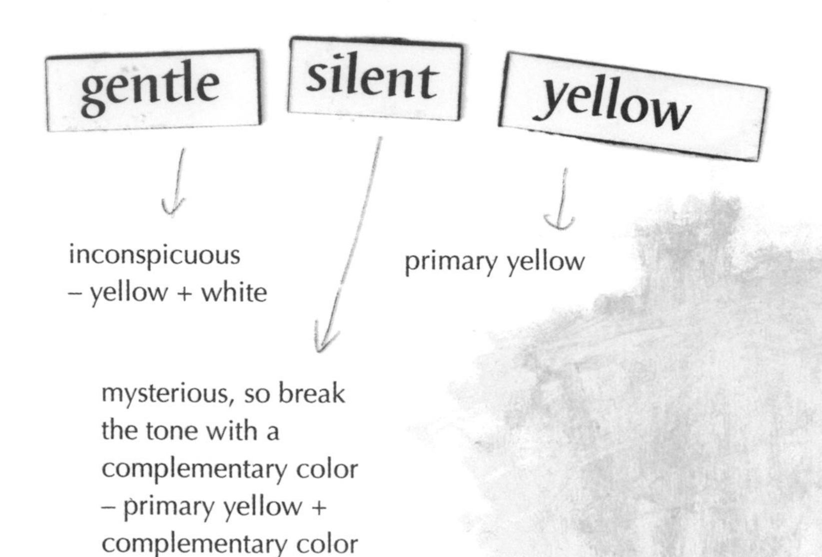
gentle
silent
yellow
inconspicuous
– yellow + white
primary yellow
mysterious, so break
the tone with a
complementary color
– primary yellow +
complementary color
purple

winter
garden
smart
star
thought
happy
nest
pumpkin
phone
bring
as
not
girl
child
turn
sea
flower
good
family
wing
pull
wrote
wish
monster
storm

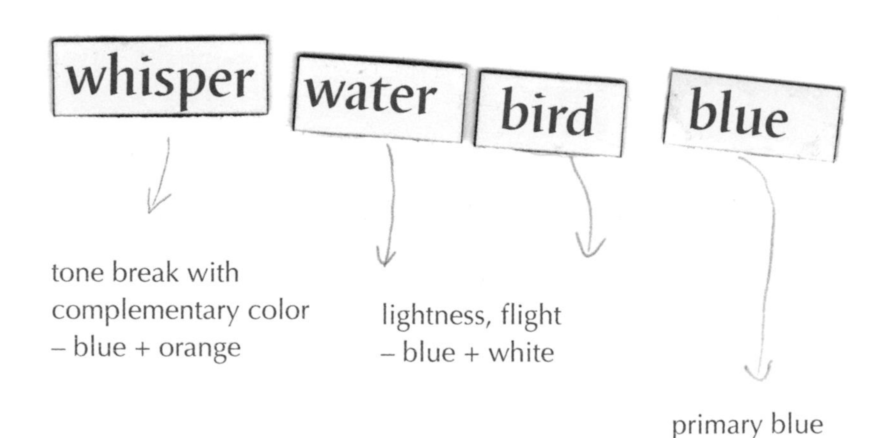

By the way, if you don't know how to make the basic colors, you may want to go to the next section, which gives you practical tips on how to make them, and how to work with complementary colors. You can then come back to this section.

The Basics

7 The Basics

So far we've been talking about how you can relate to colors, in a personal way. This can be a very exciting journey, if you want to get to know colors.

But at the same time, we all know that colors have certain qualities – they have characteristics, and they behave in a particular way with each other. If you get to know the basics of this system, you will be in control of how you use colors, and free to decide what you will do with them.

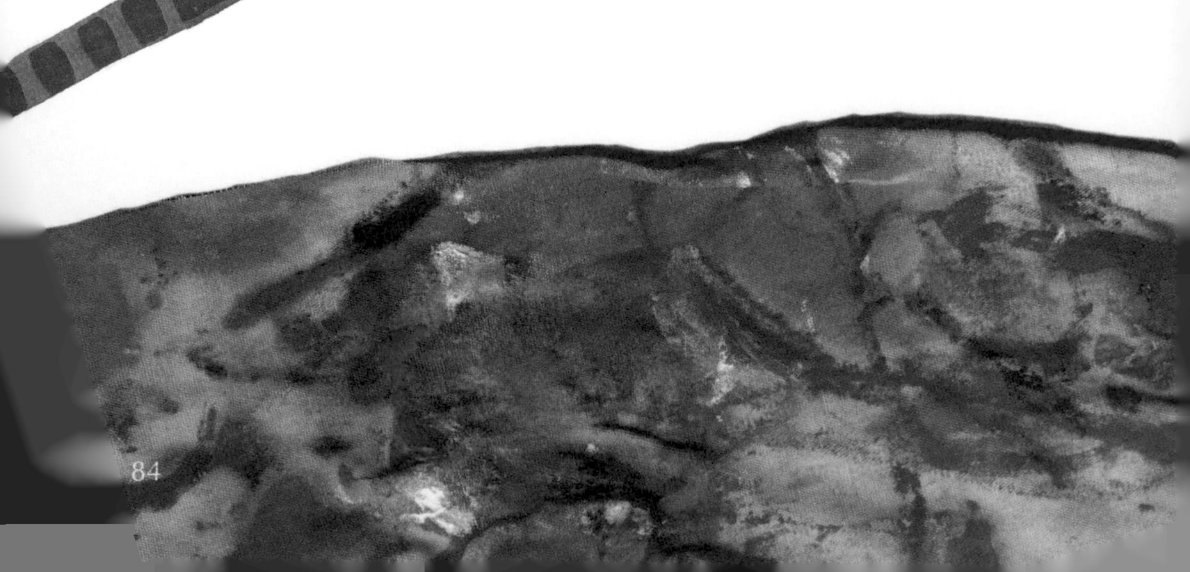

7. Primary Colors

To start using colors, get two glasses of water. One for rinsing your brush, after you have finished with a color – and as you go on, you will notice that the water becomes murky. Change it after a while.

But the other glass of clear water is for diluting a color, after you have rinsed your brush. It is important to mix the right amount of water into the color – whether you are using a paintbox, a pallete or the lid of a jar of color. The result should be easy to spread, and not too watery.

You need a piece of cloth with which you can remove excess water.

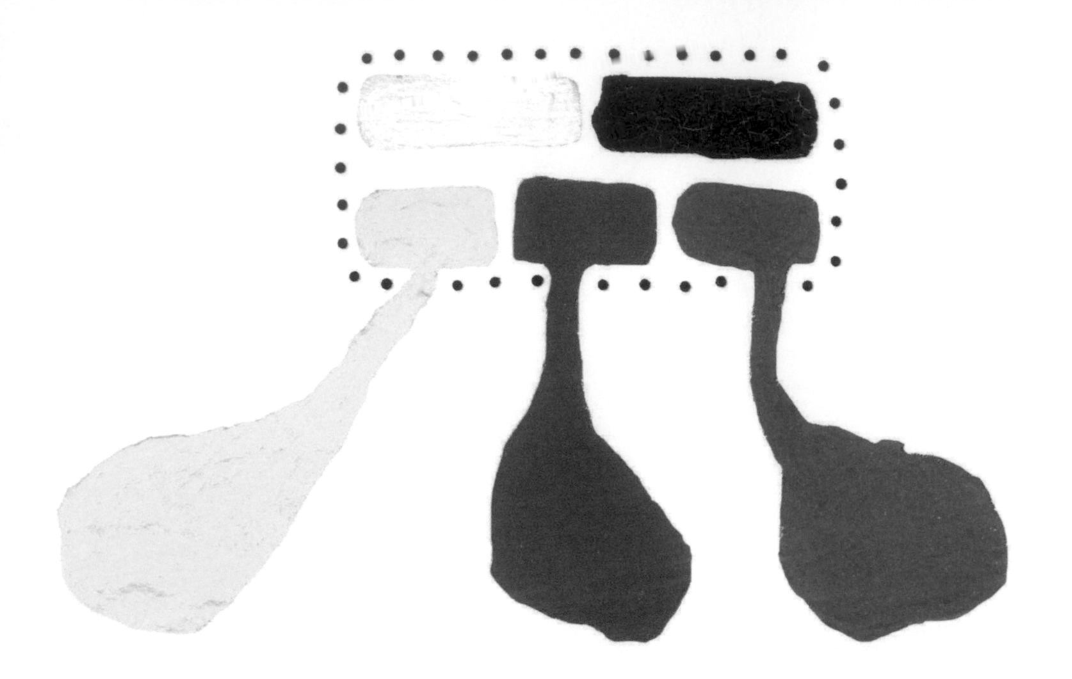

The basic colors are called PRIMARY COLORS.
They are YELLOW, RED and BLUE. In addition to these, you need WHITE and BLACK.

From these, you can make SECONDARY COLORS:

The blue, yellow and red are variable in any given color – some have more and some have less of each.

A color can be muted by gradually adding white.
See what happens when you add a bit of black to a color.
Some colors start to look a bit weird...

7.2 Complementary Colors

There is another way of making a color less brilliant, of breaking it up. You can mix it with its complementary color.

Complementary colors don't have a primary color in common. So the complementary color for...

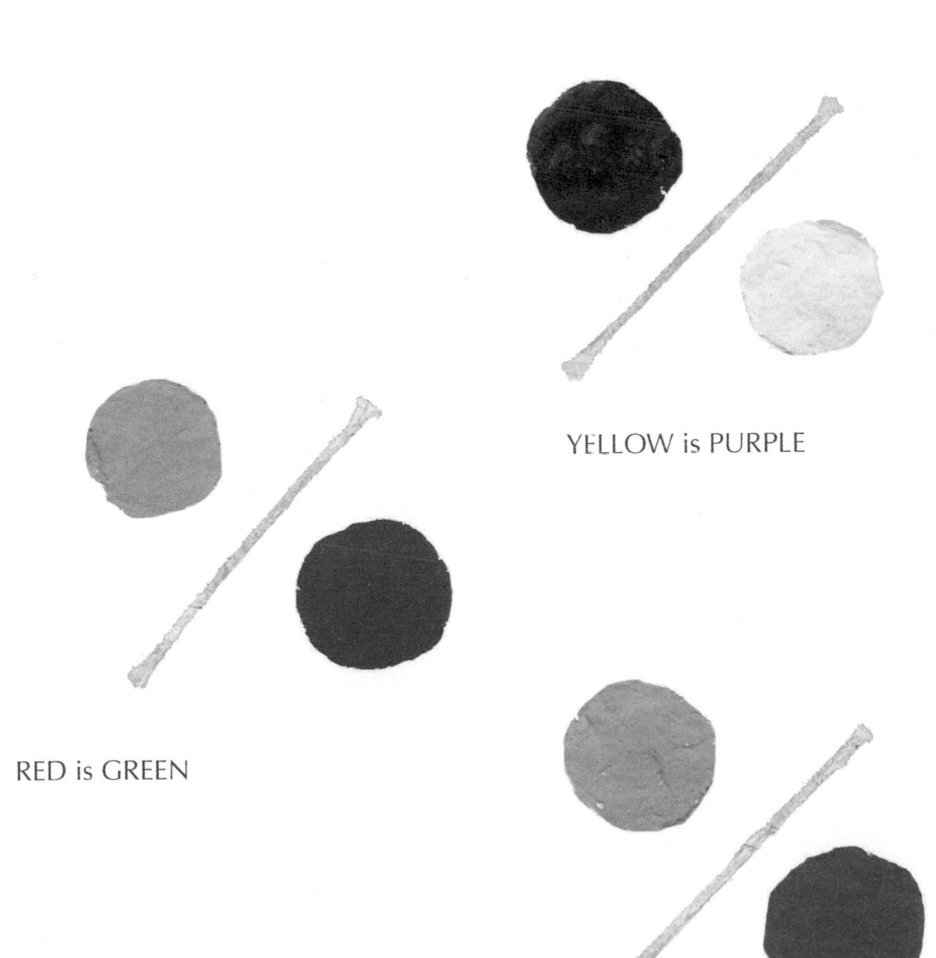

YELLOW is PURPLE

RED is GREEN

BLUE is ORANGE.

If you mix complementary colors together, you get shades of muddy brown.

But if you put complementary colors right next to each other, as you'll see from the illustration, each color appears more vivid. They enhance each other when they don't touch.

We also talk of colors as WARM or COOL.

Red, yellow and orange are warm shades...

while blue and green are cool. If you tune into the sensation of warmth or cold, you c

So if you're looking to paint a light shade, take a bit of white first, and slowly add the ot x colors very sensitively, and get the exact shade you want.

Be careful with some colors though, they dominate others.

or until you have the shade you want. If you do it the other way, you won't get a clear result.

With experience, and keeping these basic principles in mind, you'll be able to make out what a particular color is made of. And you will also be able to make the color you want, quite precisely.

7.3 Color Shade Recipes

Colors are not just different from each other – within each color, there are an infinite number of shades.

To show you how this works, I've created some charts made of color shells, with possible shades using primary colors. And this is just the beginning of what is possible!

7.3.1 Yellow

The basic color yellow is the largest shell.
Shells 1 to 10 show you what happens when you keep adding increasing drops of white to a shell.

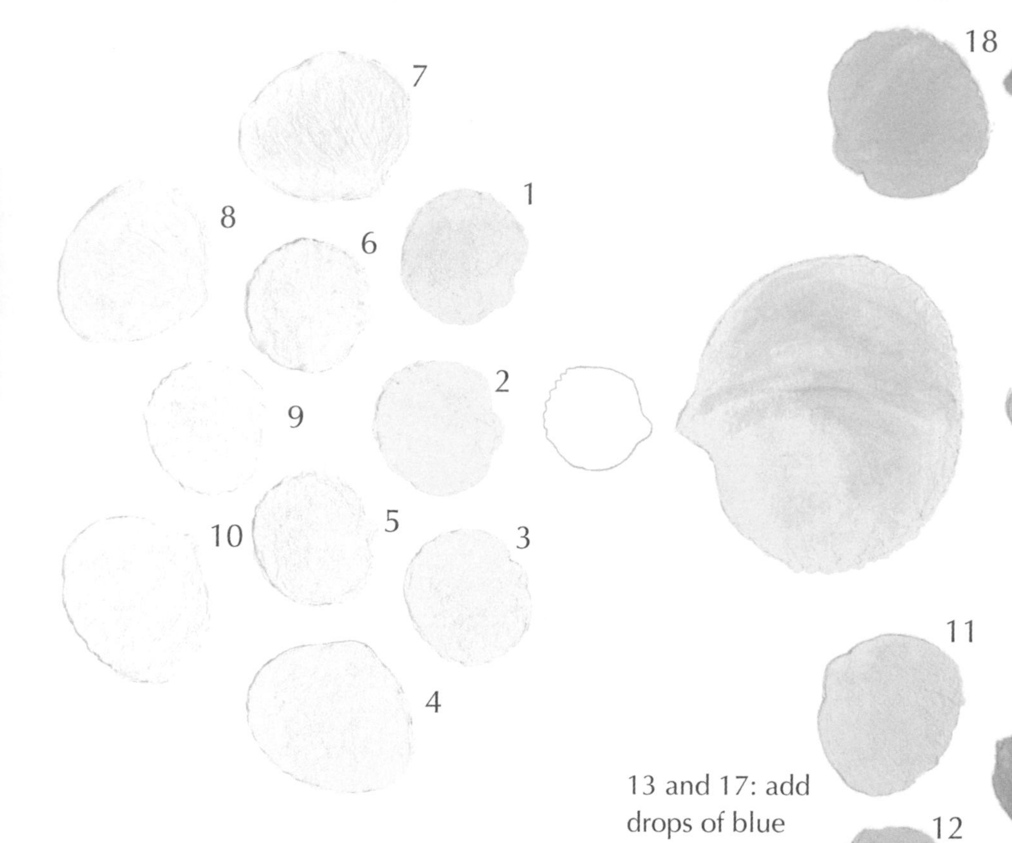

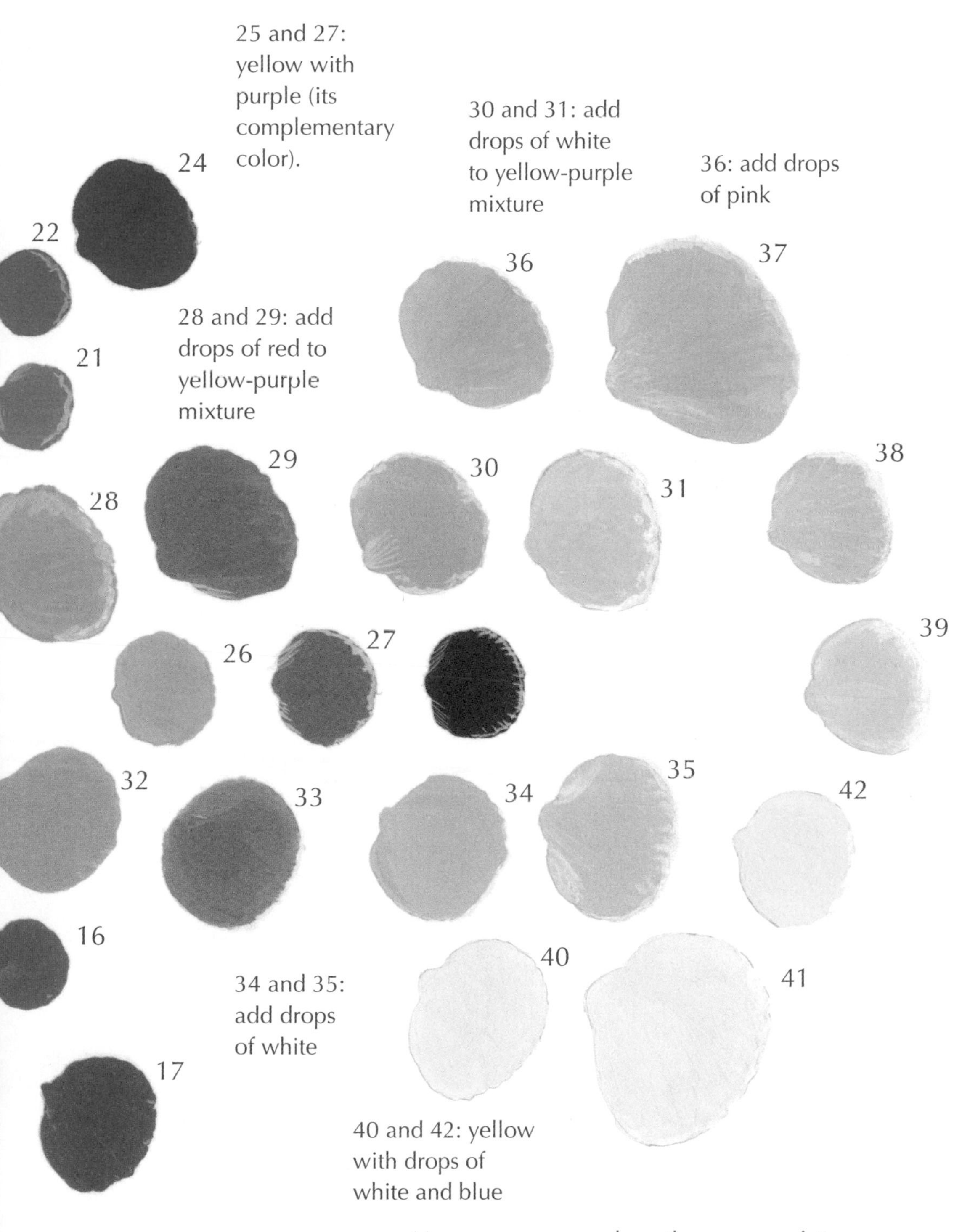

Now can you guess how these are made?
37: salmon 41: acquamarine 32: olive green
11: lemon yellow 23: vermillion

7.3.2 Red

The largest shell is red.

Shells 1 to 10 show you what happens when you add increasing drops of white to red.

18 and 24: add drops of purple and blue

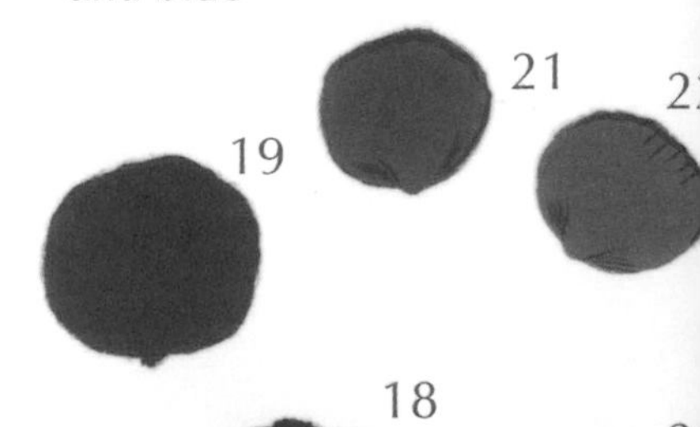

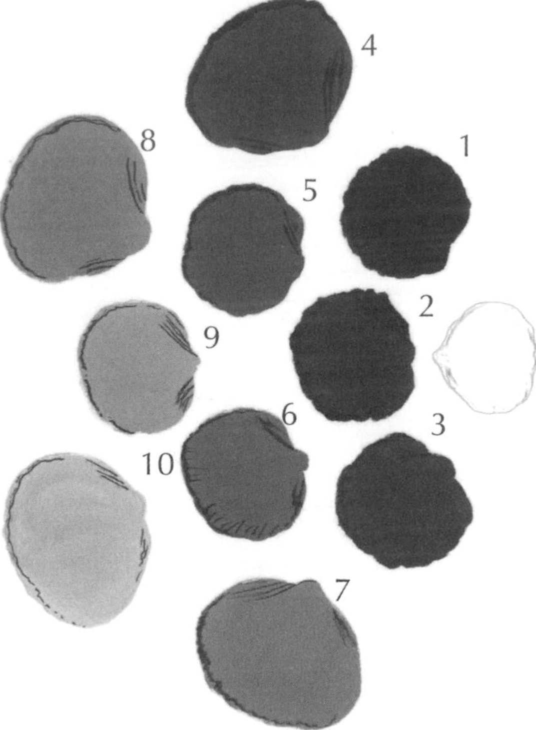

1 to 10: to red, add drops of white = pink

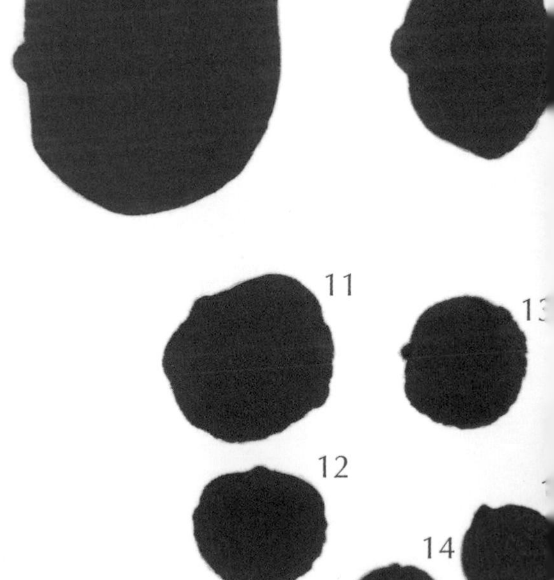

11 and 17: add drops of blue

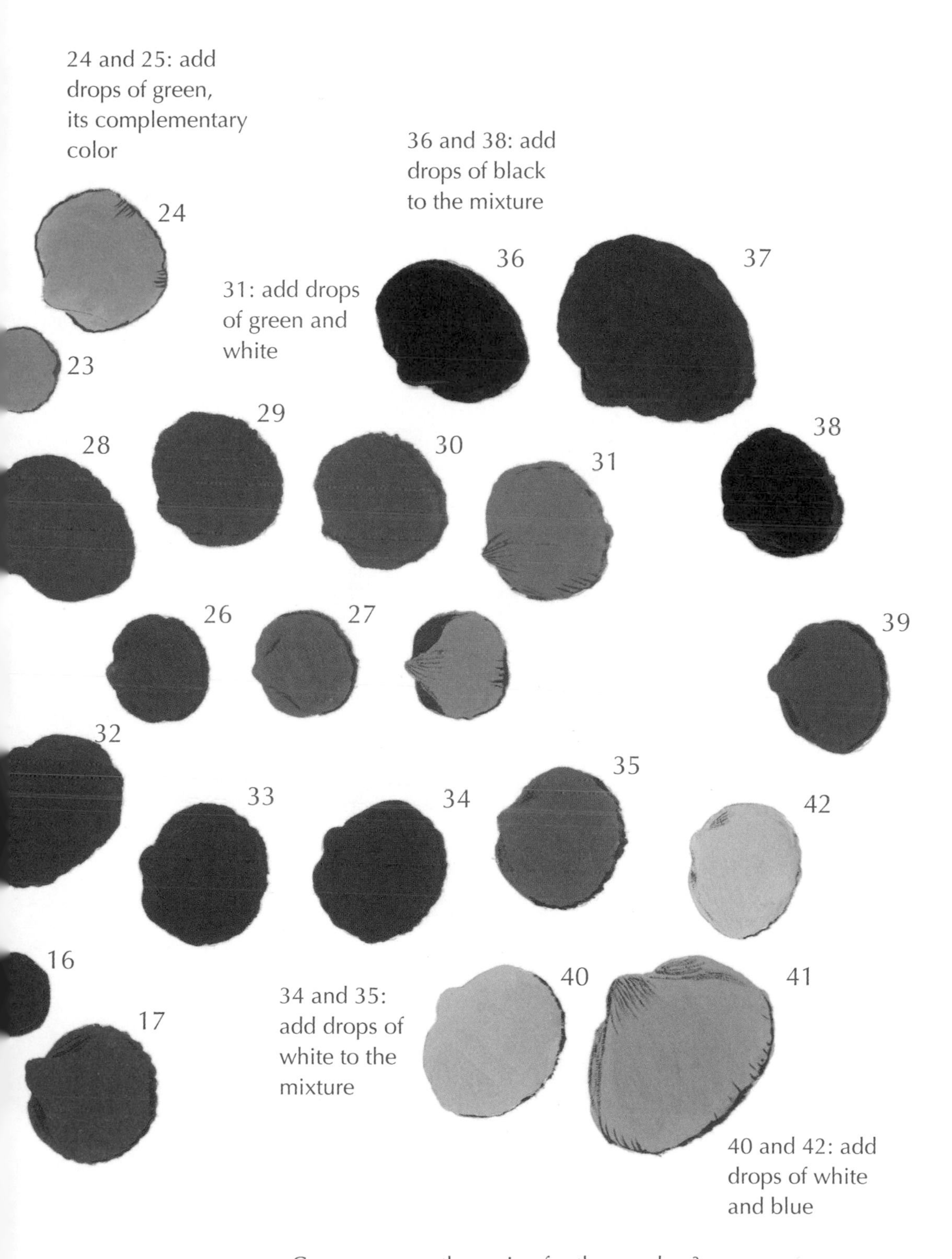

Can you guess the recipe for these colors?
39: mauve 22: orange 27: gray 37: brown 30: rust

7.3.3 Blue

The largest shell is a primary blue.

Again, shells 1 to 10 show you what happens when you add increasing drops of white to blue.

18 and 24: add drops of yellow

23

19

18

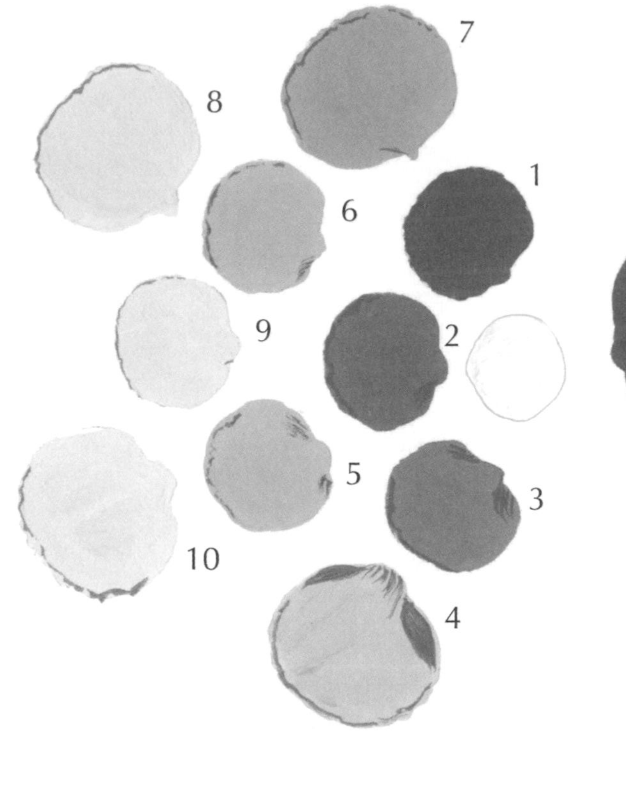

11

12

14

Now guess how these colors are created:
37: blue indigo 42: ultramarine
14: aubergine 21: pea-green
Can you name the color of shell 35?
Boiled aubergine? Pale violet?

11 and 17: add drops of red

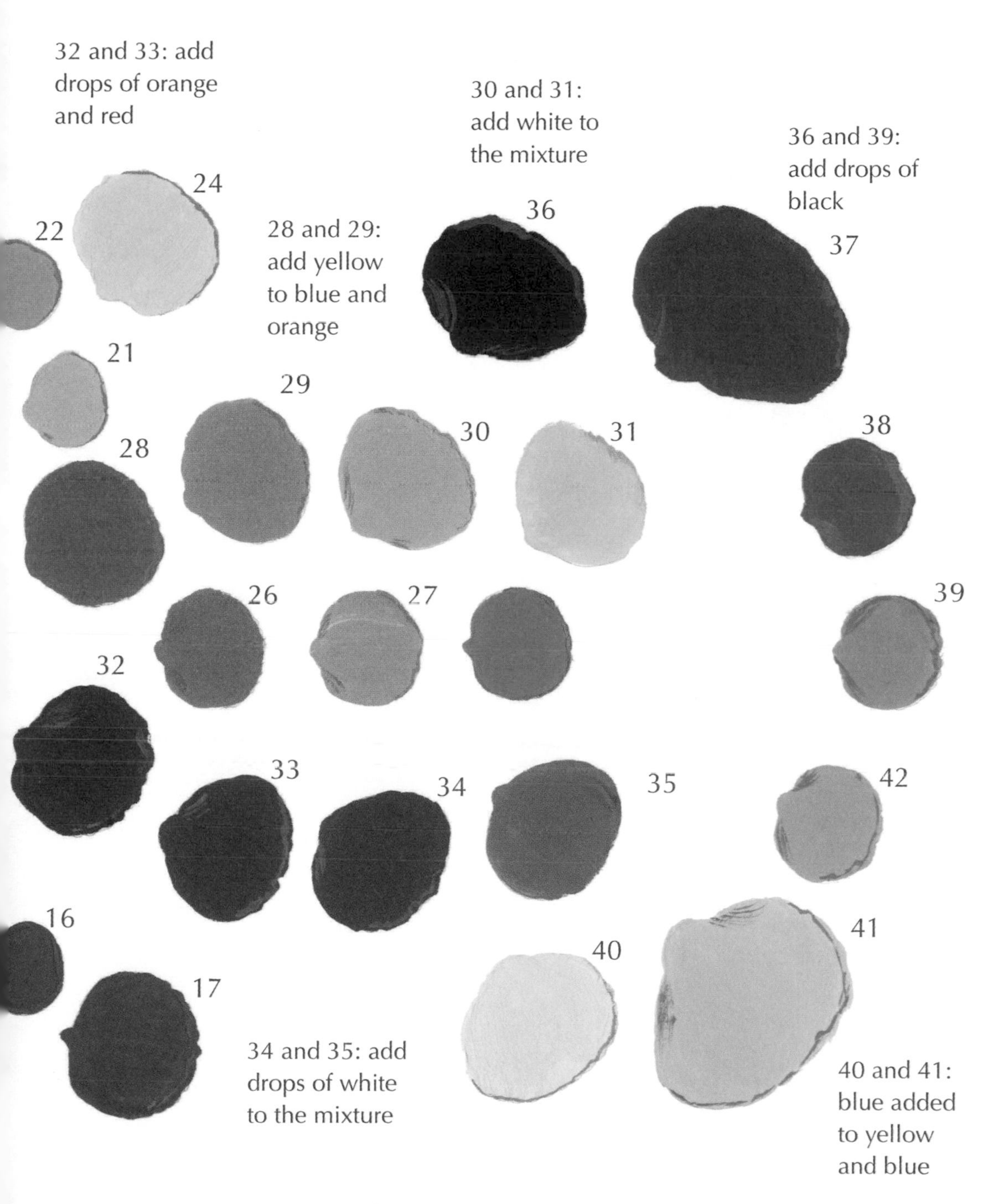

Now that you have seen how you can move towards a certain direction by slowly adding a few drops of color, we can try to make a color together.

7.4 Making a Color From Scratch

Now that you've seen how to make shades by adding a drop of color, let's make one together.

Get your two glasses of water ready, and a hard surface, like a pallete, to mix your colors. We're going to use the primary colors – yellow, red and blue – along with white. If you want, you could have green, orange and purple ready as well, but you don't need to, because you already know how these are made.

Maybe you want some black, but I'd rather you're careful, black can really ruin your mixing. I much prefer to use a brown – Burnt Umber – instead of black.

The main thing is that you need to keep these colors separate and clean, not smudging or going into each other. Only then can you get exactly what you want.

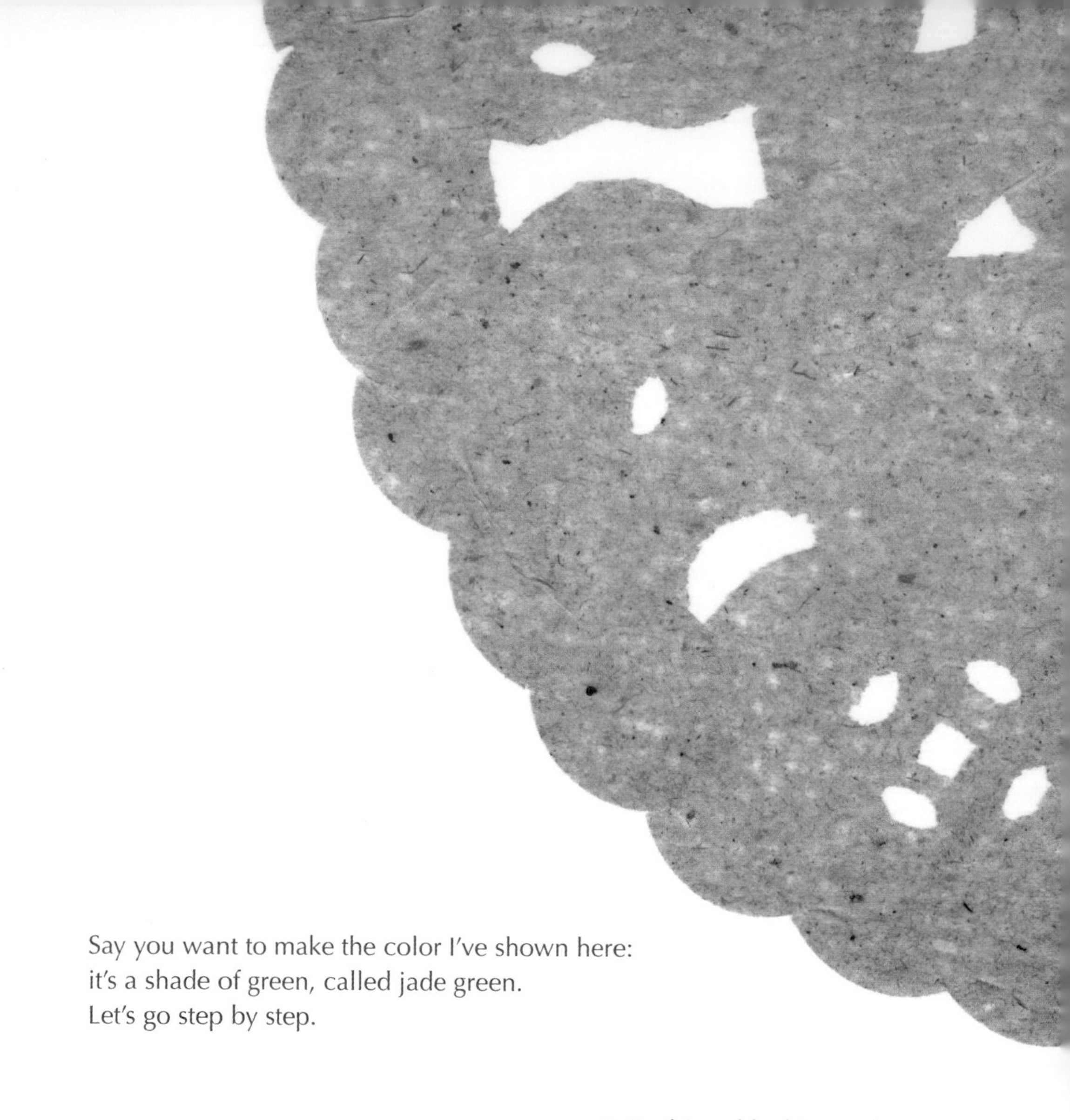

Say you want to make the color I've shown here:
it's a shade of green, called jade green.
Let's go step by step.

1. First use a base of green.
You can mix blue and yellow,
or start with a prepared green.

2. To this, add white, so it
fades a little. Then add green's
complementary color – red –
to make the shade a bit muddier,
a bit more grayish.

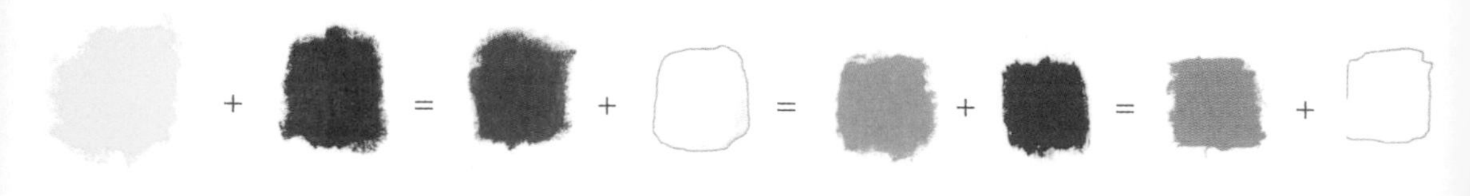

primary yellow

primary blue

green

white

red (complementary color of green)

white

3. Keep adding a bit of white, if you want it to fade, or increase the green, until you get the jade color you want.

4. If you look closely at the shade of jade green I've made, you can see that the base is clear, but there are darker spots on it.
Can you guess how I did that?

8 Your Own Color

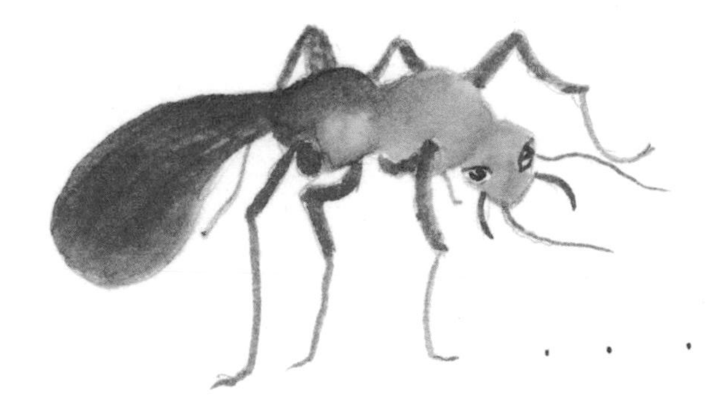

ails

Now that you know how it works, you can get to the real thing: making your own colors, using the tips I gave you. Be bold and patient – you're like an ant, with the same spirit of adventure.

Start with the primary colors: you should know them well by now. YELLOW, RED and BLUE

8.1 Your Color Maze

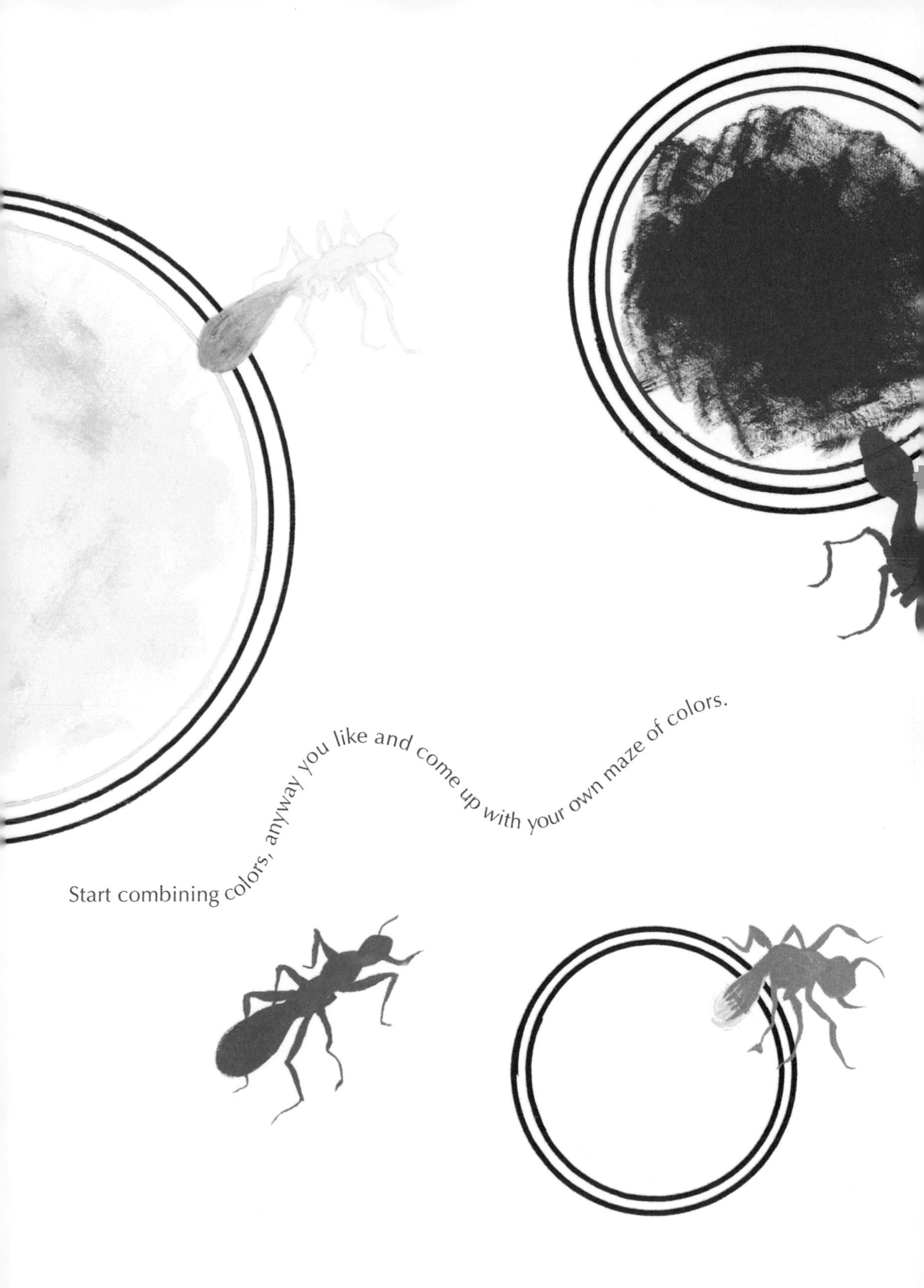
Start combining colors, anyway you like and come up with your own maze of colors.

Only you know how you got there, and how you can get out.

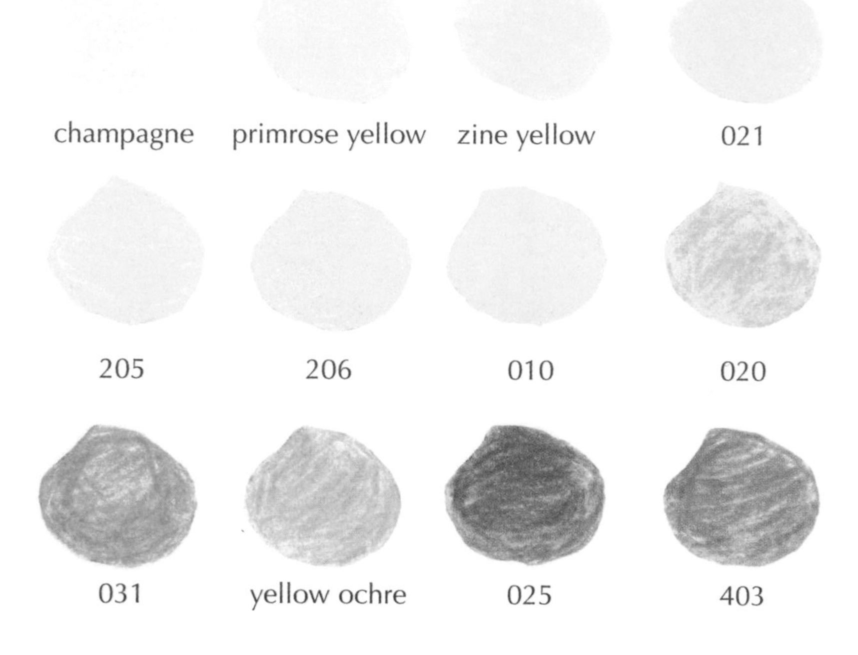

8.2 Your Own Shade System

Collect all the colors that you own – crayons, poster colors, markers, watercolors – and start arranging them around you. How you do this is up to you. You could go from yellow to gray, or have shades of blue, or contrasts next to each other.

When you buy paints, the different shades can also have names that are particular to a region: in India you could have "Peacock Blue", and in Italy "Pompeian Red." Your paint tubes or bottles can also have numbers on them and I've included the ones that mine had.

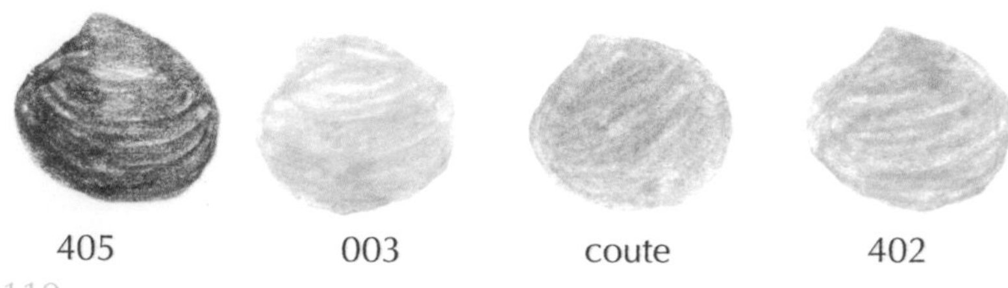

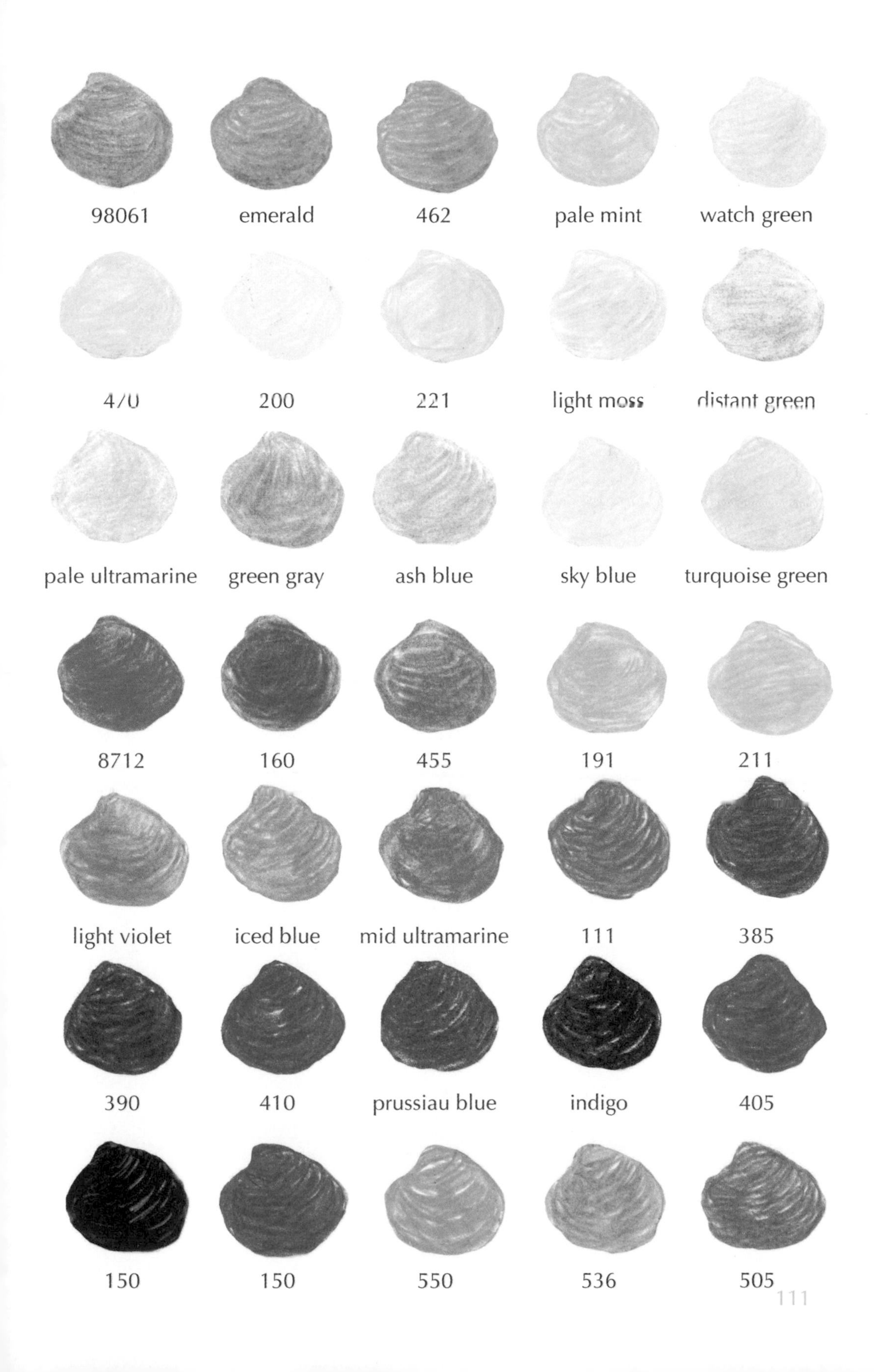
98061
emerald
462
pale mint
watch green
470
200
221
light moss
distant green
pale ultramarine
green gray
ash blue
sky blue
turquoise green
8712
160
455
191
211
light violet
iced blue
mid ultramarine
111
385
390
410
prussiau blue
indigo
405
150
150
550
536
505

This is your system for today. On another day, you might choose to have a different order entirely, depending on how you feel and what you want to do. You'll realize that you enjoy coming up with your own Color Dance. It's fun to order other things according to color as well... maybe your collection of shells?

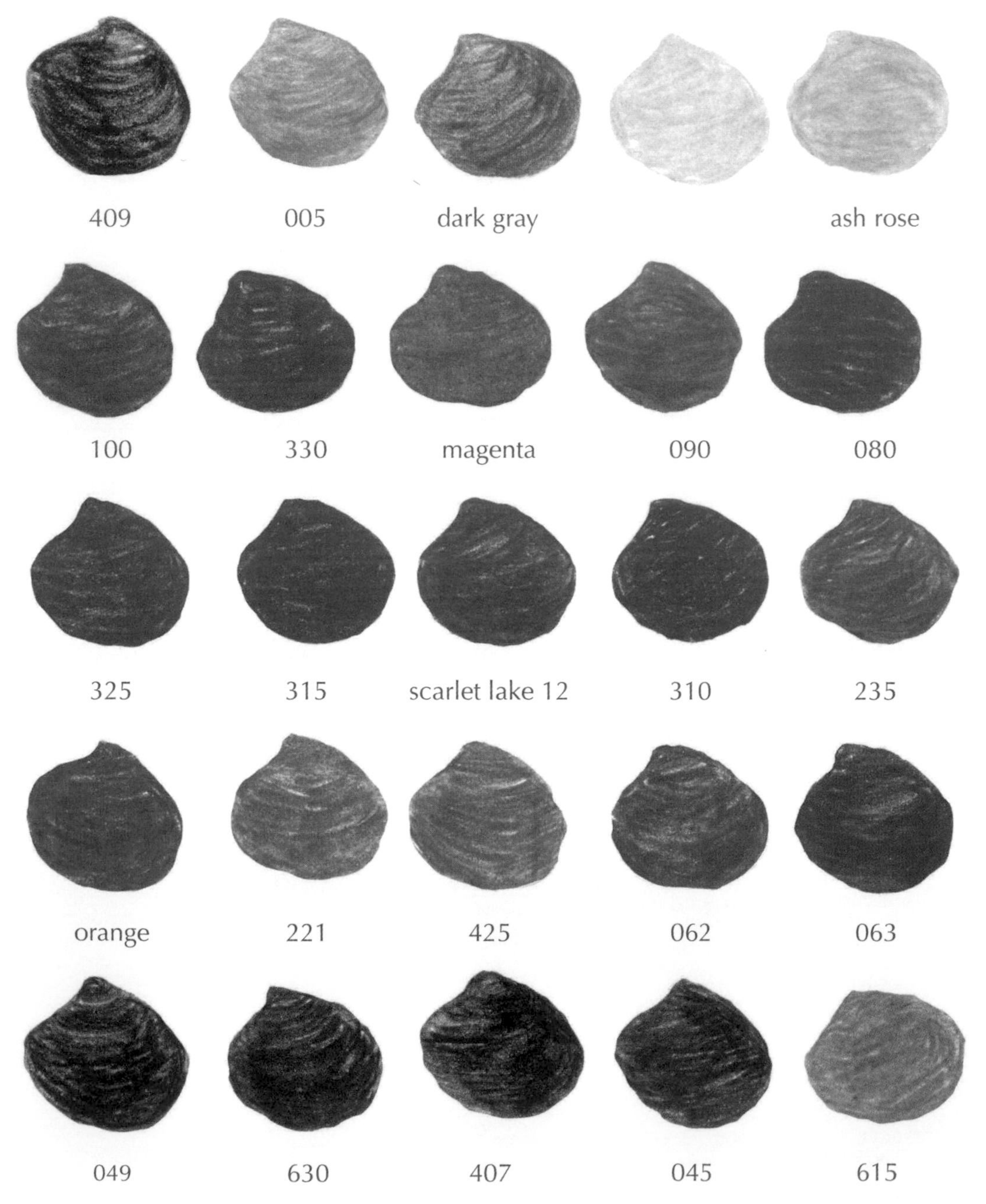

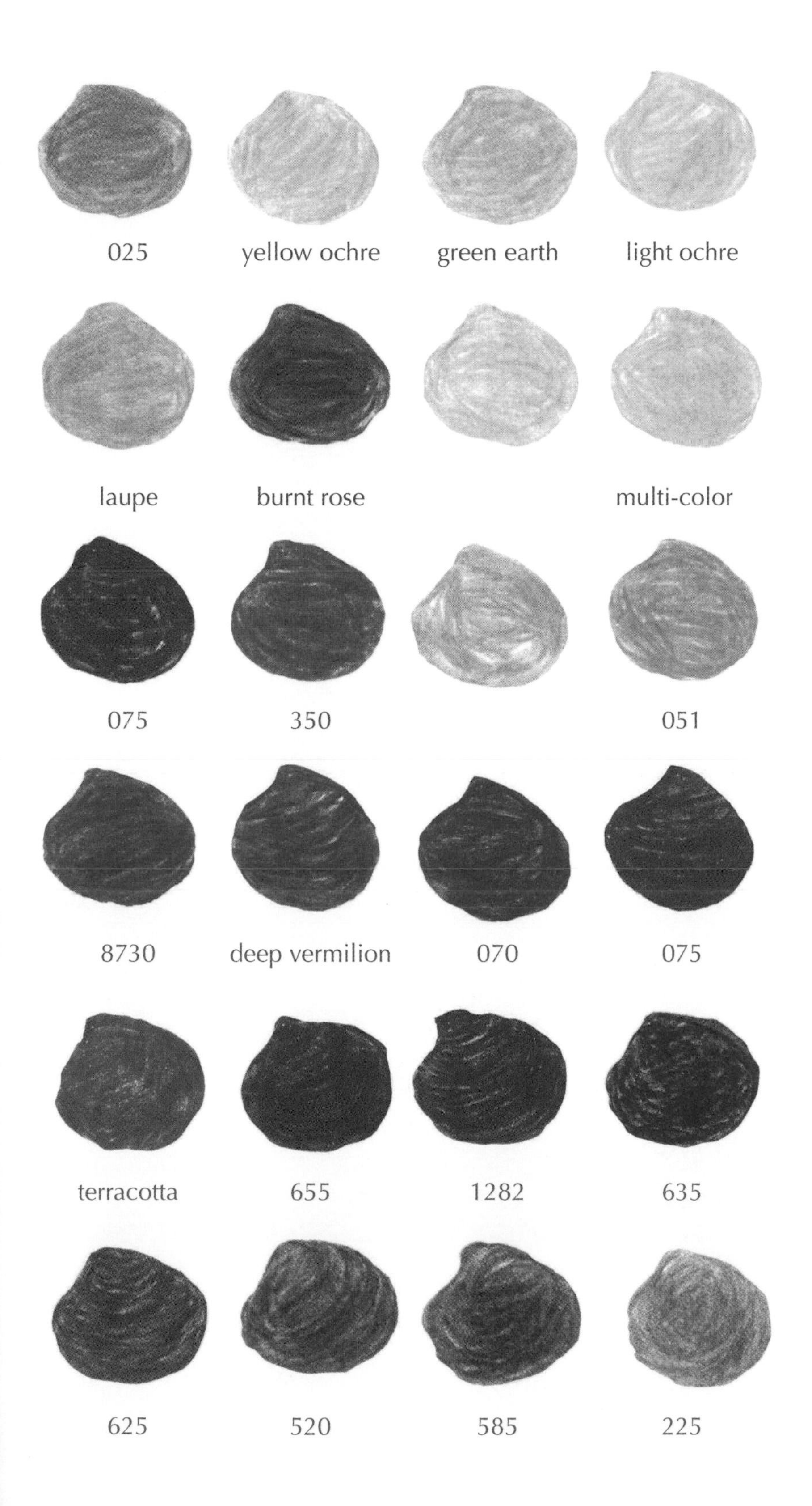
025
yellow ochre
green earth
light ochre
laupe
burnt rose
multi-color
075
350
051
8730
deep vermilion
070
075
terracotta
655
1282
635
625
520
585
225

8.3 Portrait of Your Color Box

Now that you've ordered your colors, why not paint a portrait of your color box with all the colors in it?
This exercise will help you get familiar with the colors, their shades, and make a kind of color map for you to refer to.

You can make a different map for each kind of color you choose –

one for poster colors, for instance,

one for crayons, one for colored pencils etc.

You could also choose a shape, like the way I've chosen the shell, and paint into this shape.

Remember to write the name of the color against the shade.

Permanent Green Light
Primary Blue
Turquoise Blue
Sky blue
Indigo
Ultramarine Deep
Vert Olive
Rich Green Deep
A MADRE
Helio Green bluish
Linden Green
Gris Jaune
Cobalt Violet Light

FABBRIC
VIA CAPO
Brown Pink
BIB
MONTANA
English Red
ARK
Burnt Umber
Primary Yellow
CASA DI S. M.
ROMA
Umberto No. 173
Persian Yellow Medium
SI COM
Sig
ER RIFERI
RE AL DER
Pres
PUTATO
RENZIS
CA
Corso
ente

9 Your New Eyes

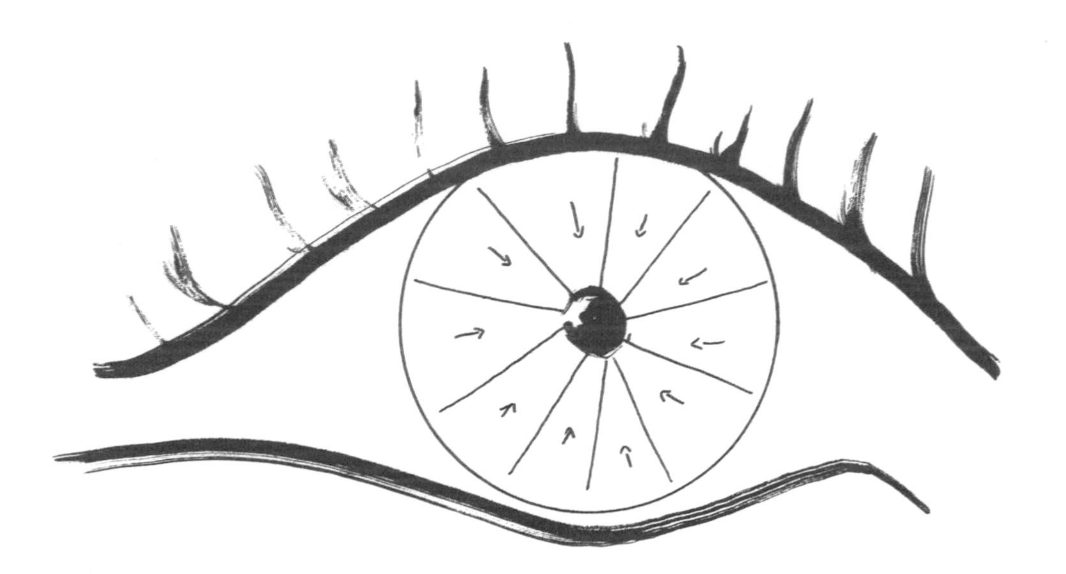

Now that you're familiar with color shades, try this: draw an eye, like the one here, on a sheet of paper. Divide the iris into rays. Then gather some magazines together, and cut out shades of color that are similar to each other.

You need two shapes for each shade – a square, and a ray like in the iris.

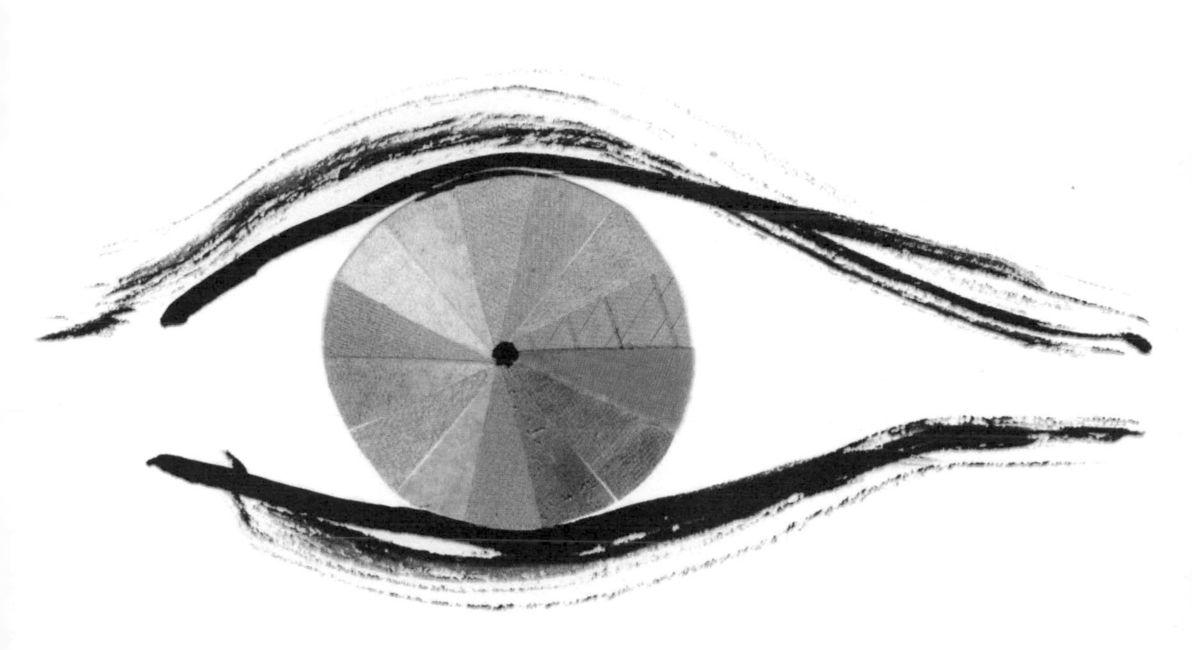

Arrange the ray-shaped paper in a harmonious order around the iris, and paste them in. Paste the square bits of paper in the same order under the eye (you can go in clockwise or counter-clockwise order around the iris rays).

Now comes the challenging part.

Next to each bit of paper, work out how you might make this color, like I have done.

Once you've done that, draw the other eye on a different sheet of paper, and once again divide the iris into rays.

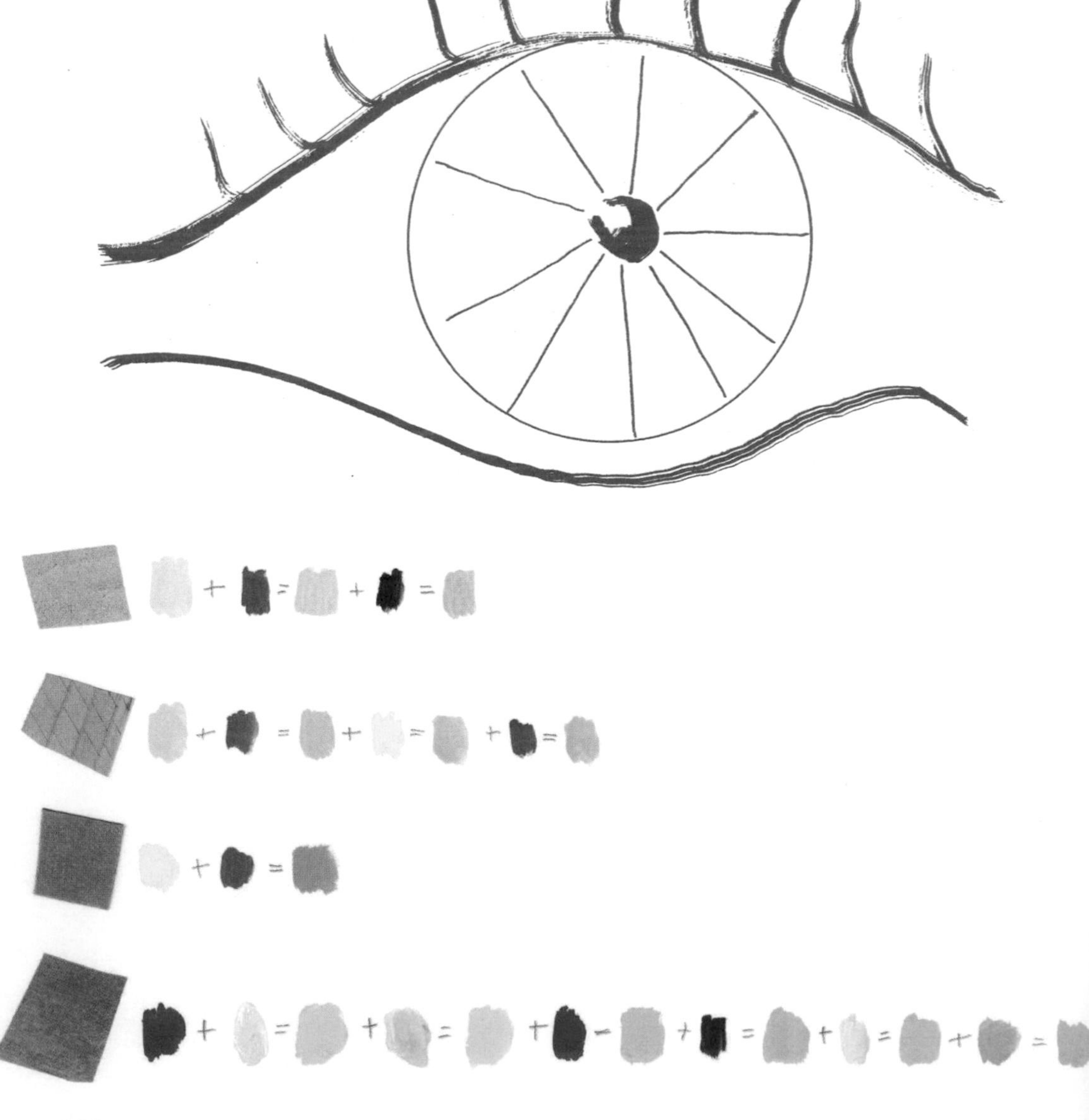

This time, instead of pasting in shades of paper, actually paint the rays in exactly the same shades, in the same order, as the left iris.

The colors will of course look slightly different, but satisfy yourself that you've matched it as much as possible. Finding a color is always a revelation!

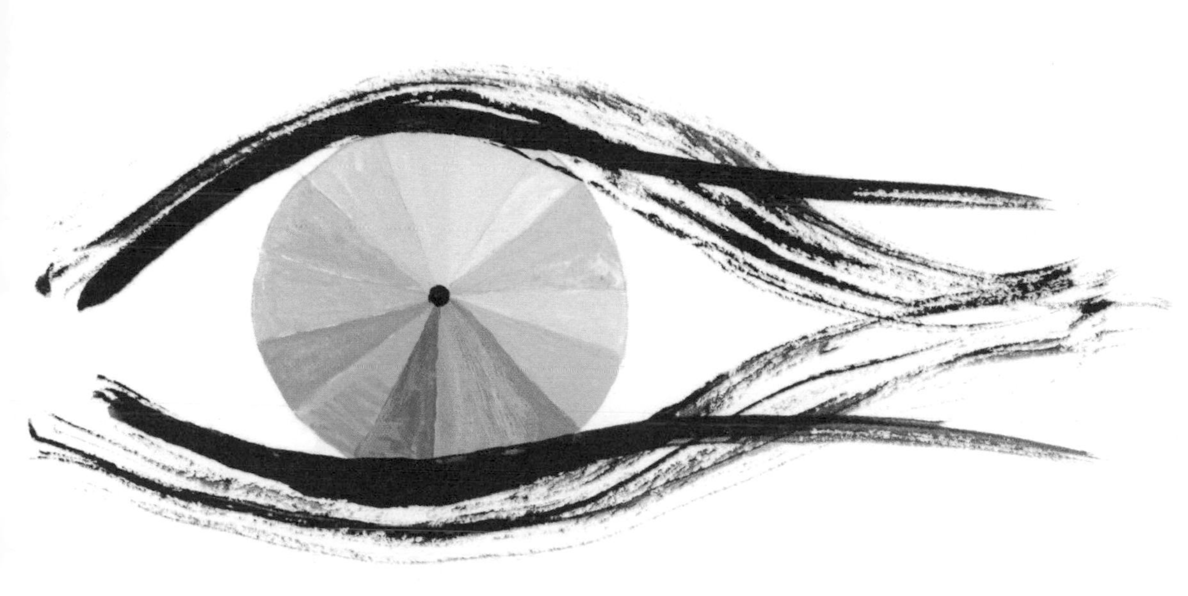

Once you're able to do this, you really have your own personal vision of colors. It's a great feeling.

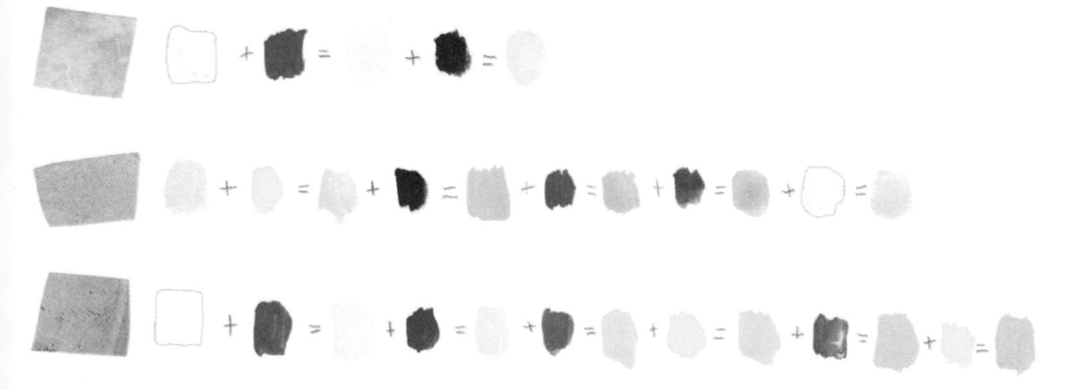

10 Matching Colors

10.1 Harmony & Contrasts

When you're working with colors, it's important to keep in mind that it's good to keep some distance, a bit of "breathing space" between them. These "non-colored" spaces are crucial to the way we see and experience colors – so when you assemble colors, you're really working with colored and non-colored spaces.

The second thing to note is the effect that particular colors have when they're placed next to each other. Some colors are enhanced by their neighbors, while others disappear shyly. There are two ways to combine colors: the first is harmony, where the colors are similar in tone, and the second is contrast, where they are the opposite of each other.

When I want to create a harmonious sequence of colors, I put a bit of the old color in the new one I'm mixing, so that there is a continuity of tone. Or I dab a bit of color on one side of the paper, and a dab on the opposite side as well, to keep the whole thing together. You can try your own ways of creating harmony.

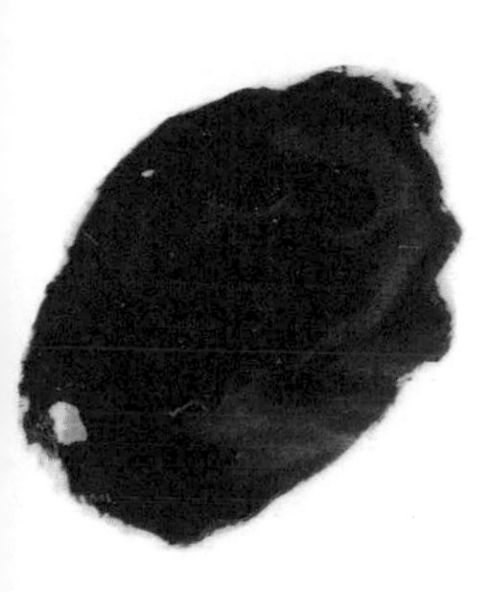

On the other hand, if you love contrasts, try putting complementary colors next to each other. They not only stand out from each other, but seem to literally emerge from the paper.

Matching colors, putting them side by side, is an art. Look at how this happens in nature, or in the city, in art from different parts of the world, at things around you: clothes, rooms... every culture has its own particular way of combining colors.

Even within the same culture, individual people have their own preferences. My favorite combination for years has been red or orange with purple. I also love yellow with gray, as well as orange with blue.

Colors are reflected in each other, and the art of combining them is in some ways always a surprise, and always individual. I sometimes feel that you can talk about some principles, but color combinations cannot be taught, it comes almost like an instinct, and you know when you're happy with your result. So in the end, you have to come up with your own way of combining colors, which is special to you.

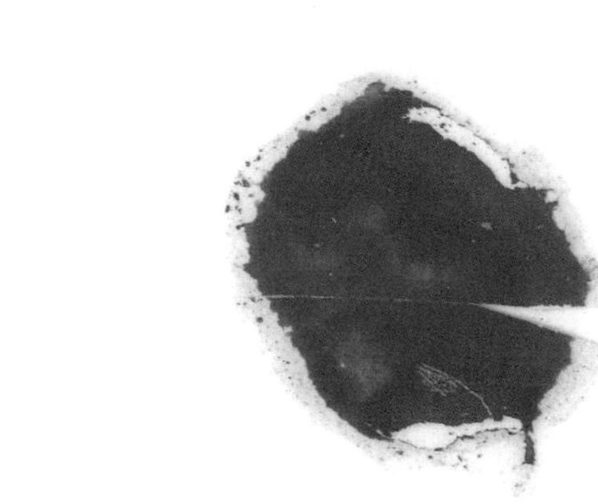

If there is one basic quality you need to combine colors, it is DARING. Don't be afraid, be easy about trying your hand at harmony, as well as contrast.

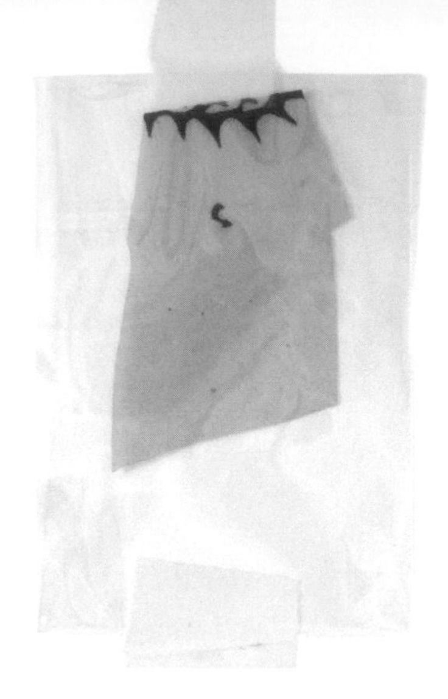

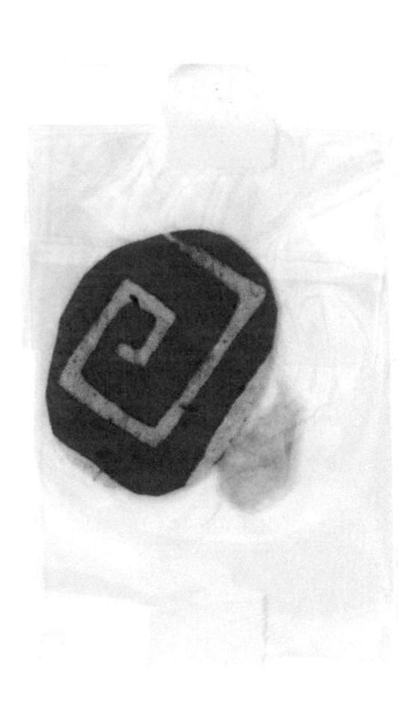

Here's a fun way to practice matching colors. Buy some small plastic envelopes, and in each one of them, put in different little colored objects: pieces of cloth, paper, wire, a picture, a photograph of a dress, a pressed flower, a ticket, photos of color, of paintings...

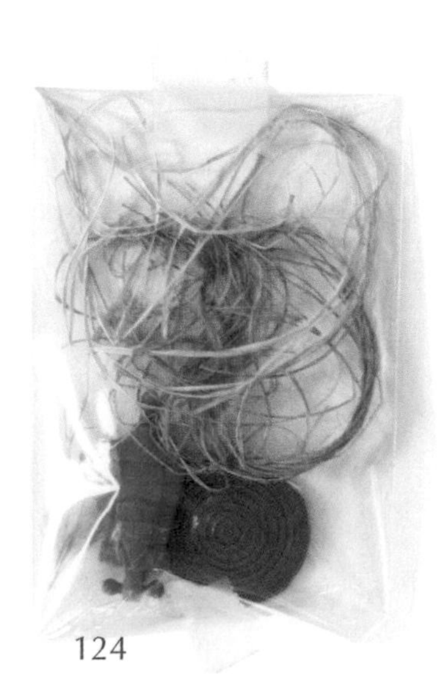

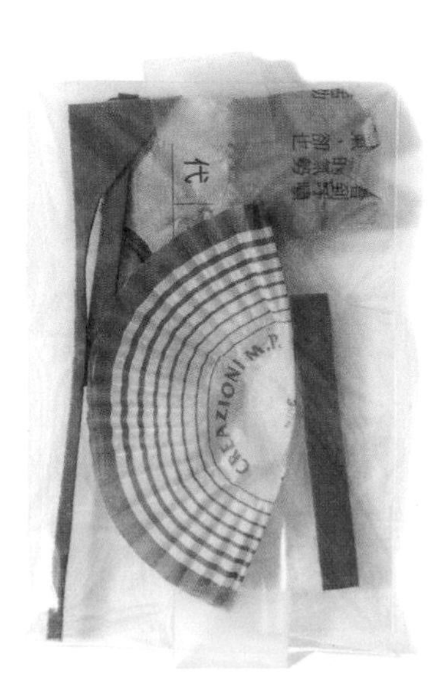

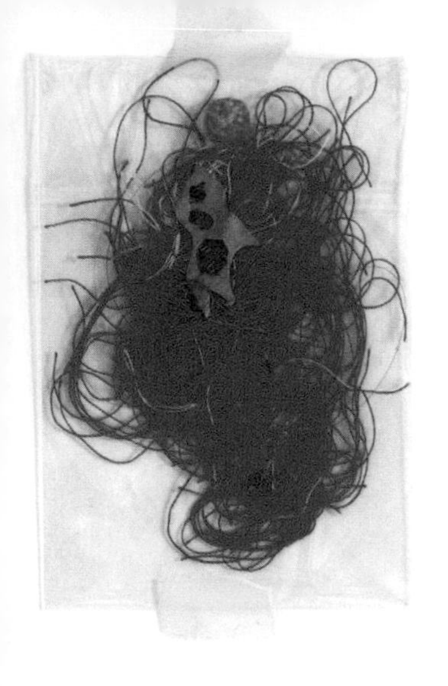

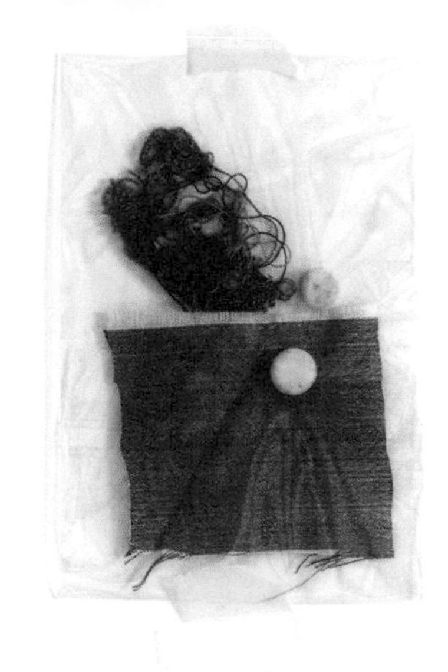

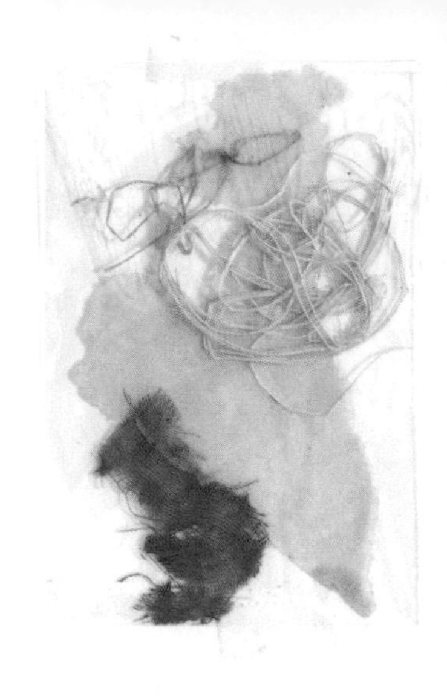

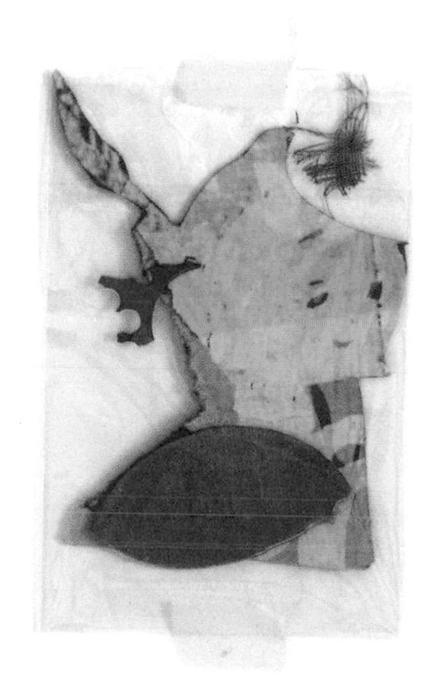

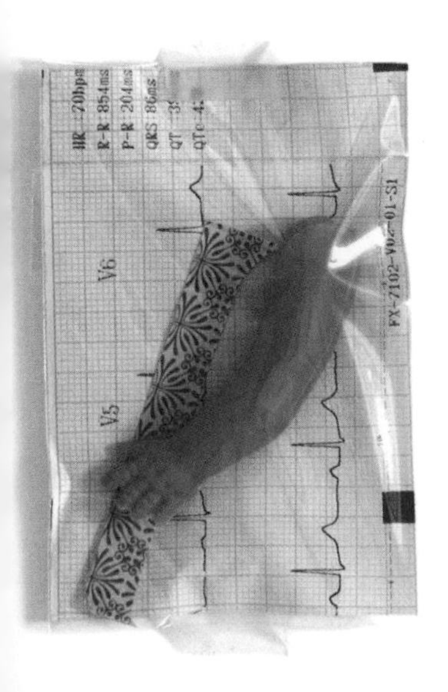

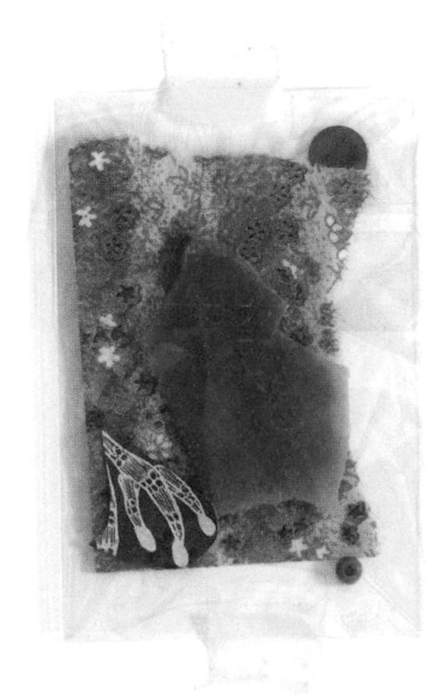

These are your little idea pouches, for color combinations. With these ideas, you can start on a more ambitious project: a book of color.

– 106 years old

– 55 years old

– 30 years old

– 25 years old

– 12 years old

– 9 years old

– 6 years old

11 Your Own Book of Color

The Color Dance, our little dance around color, has now brought us to a point – this is where you need to continue your experience with color by yourself.

A great way to do this is to begin on a book that will grow with you, a book that records colors and feelings for you, as they change and develop.

You've probably seen small sample color swatches that paint shops have. For your book, I'm not thinking of this kind of thing so much as something very personal, more like the kind of book where people preserve pressed leaves and herbs. Your book will be your personal collection of everything to do with color – from your color box to recording feelings and sensations...
it could be images, objects, photographs, paintings...
anything that records your own Color Dance.

11.1 Making The Book

You need

Lots drawing paper – you'll just use one side of each sheet
Masking tape
Colored ribbon
Two pieces of cardboard
Glue
Scissors
Watercolors
Poster colors
Colored pencils
Markers

To make your never-ending book, you need to fold sheets of paper in the middle, and tape the edges together like an accordion. If you look carefully at the illustration here, you'll see how it's made. You would only use one side of the paper.

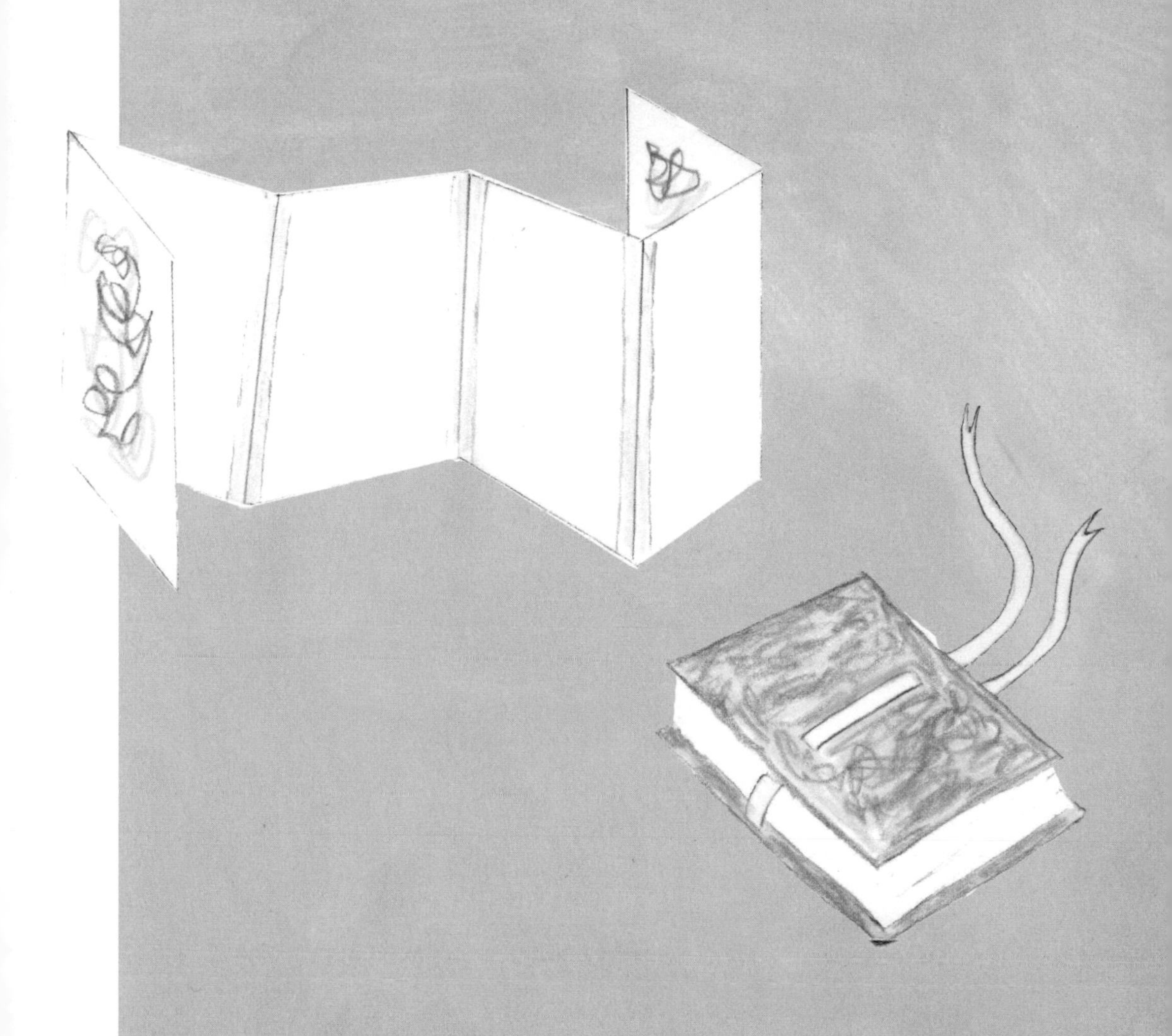

For the cover, take two pieces of cardboard which are slightly larger than the sheets of paper. Make slits on the side as shown, and draw a ribbon through them. You'll be placing the accordion book between the covers, and tying it together with a nice bow.

Over time, you can keep adding more 'pages' to your book, by gluing them in to the last page. Just stretch the tape on the cover, as the pages increase and your book becomes thicker. Your book will grow with you.

If you know already what you want to put into your book, go right ahead; if you're wondering where to start, though, I have some suggestions for you to begin.

11,2 A Palette of Memories

Do you remember talking about the colors we remember from childhood? Go to page 12 to refresh yourself, and then start writing down the memories you have of a color.

Try to use your best handwriting, and if you like, colored marker pens.
Think about...

black

green

red

blue

white

purple

yellow

pink

11,3 Magic Potions

Have you ever made magic potions out of strange things like mud, grass, dried flowers, spices? Make up different magic potion recipes, and glue them into your book.

11.4 Lists

Make a list of
all the

yellow
red
blue
orange
violet
green
white
black
things you know.

Now invent a story around each color – containing characters, objects, fruits, moods, scenes. If you need more inspiration, go back to the section which had Color Characters (page 20). I was thinking of Ms Yellow who carries a lemon in her yellow bag; or a startled blue goat whose milk is made of ink…

I'm sure you can come up with all kinds of stories, and paint them.

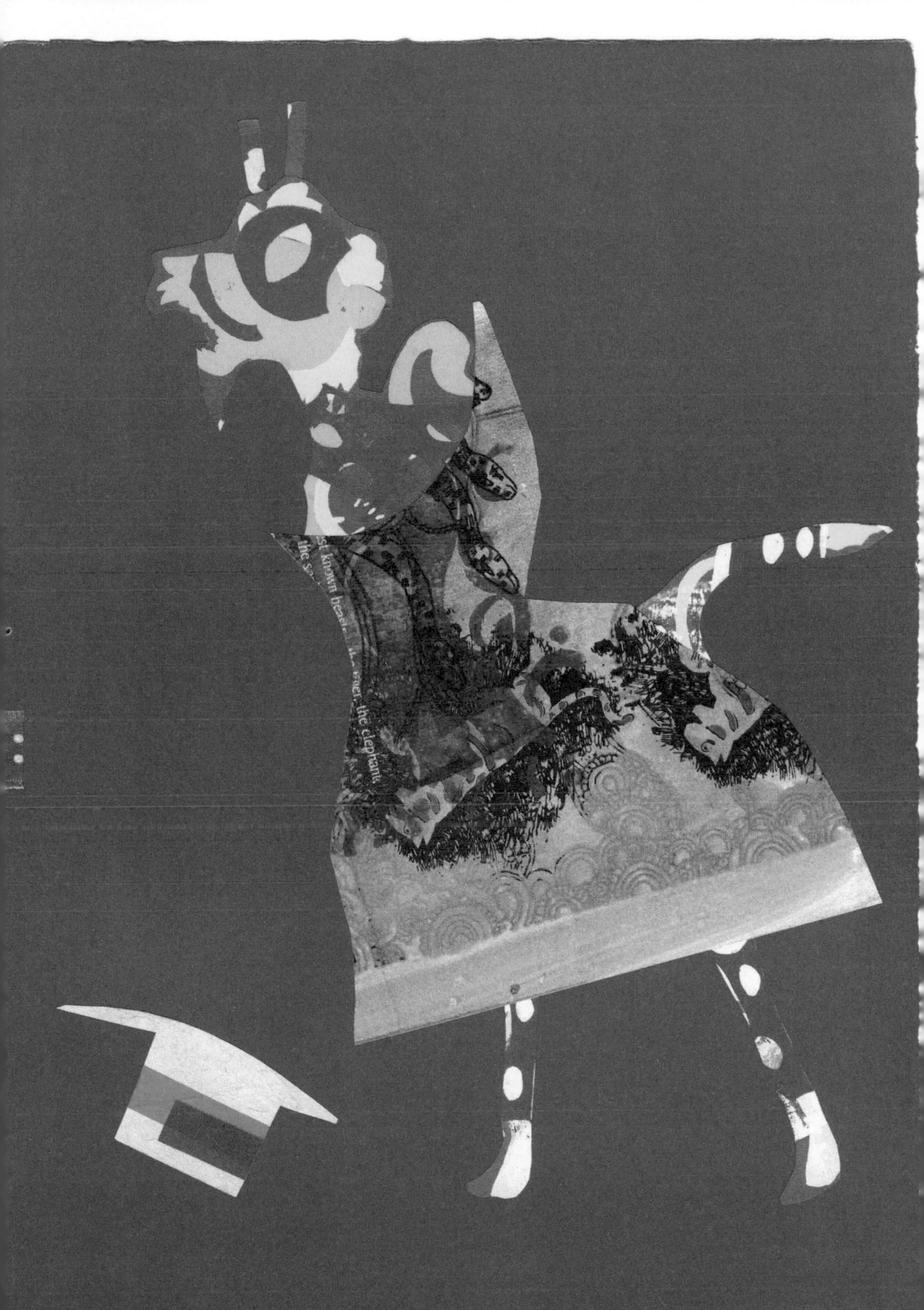
the elephant

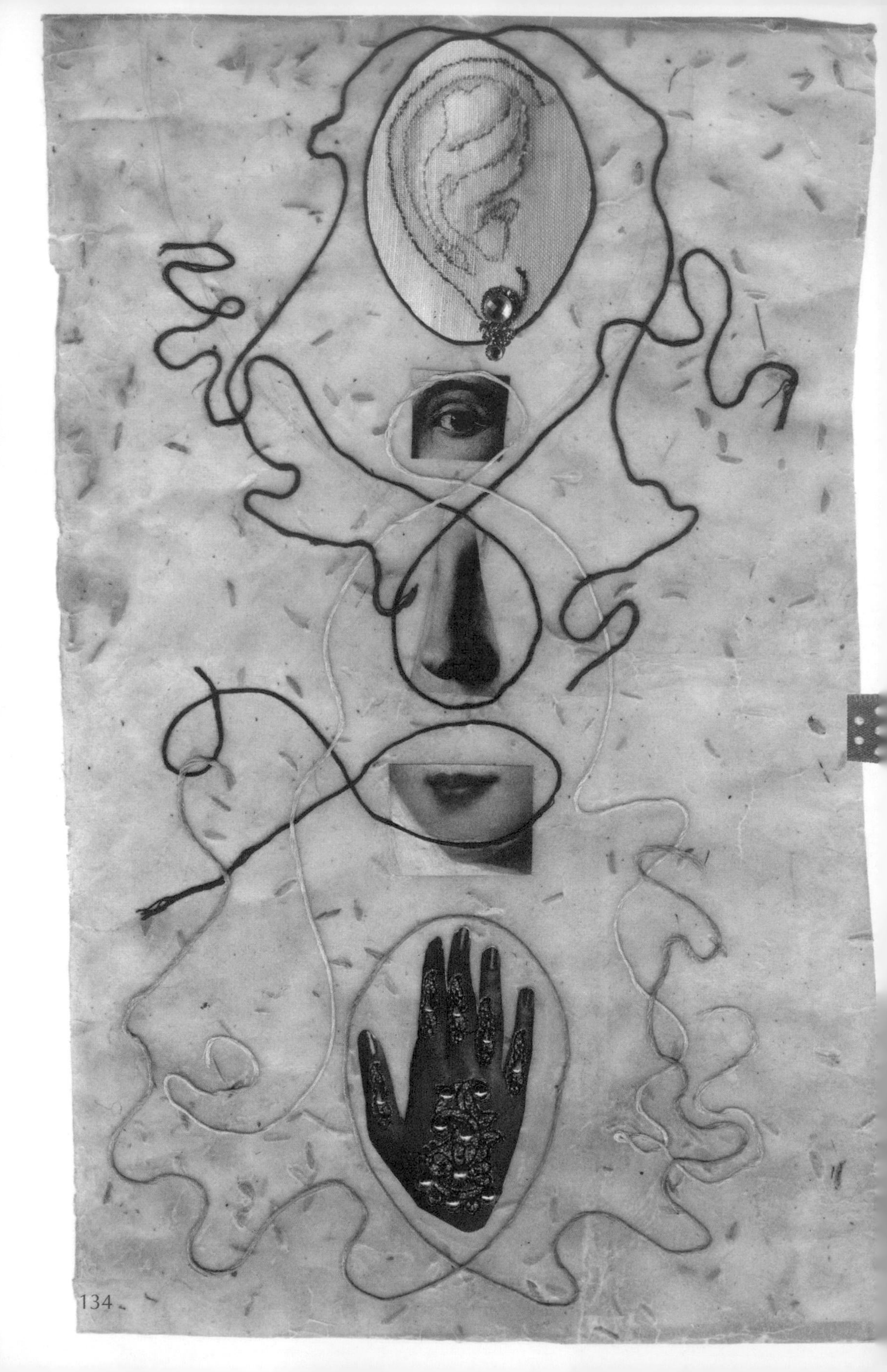

11.5 The Five Senses

Look at each of these colors – yellow, red, blue, green, orange, purple, white, black, brown, and pink – then come up with a smell, a sound, a taste and a feel for that color.

Paint each color, and write these senses down next to it.

11.6 The Hunt

You're living in a very colorful world – start exploring things around you in terms of color – in the kitchen, in your cupboard, around the house... then go out for a walk with a bag or basket and collect things – for their color. With the objects you collect, try making a small colored temple (look at the Color Forest, page 40 for more ideas).

You can also hunt for color with a camera, print these out, and paste them in your Color Book. There are probably things that strike you on your color hunt... write them down in a small notebook. For instance, you could make a note of all the shades that make up a color.

11.7 Dreams

Think of all the colors that exist, and put down the ones that make you dream or travel far away in your imagination. You can paint them as well.

11.8 Inventions

Invent colors by playing with words. For more ideas on how to do this, go to Personal Colors (page 78). Once you have the names, paint them into your book.

11.9 Quotations

Sometimes what people have said about color can be very inspiring to write down, read again, and think about. I love to collect quotations from writers or artists. Here are a few examples, I'm sure you can soon build up a list of quotations you love.

"Clouds come floating into my life, no longer to carry rain or usher storm, but to add color to my sunset sky." – Rabindranath Tagore.

"...I entered the chapel of Giotto, where the entire roof and the base of the frescoes are so blue that it looks as though the radiant day has also crossed the threshold with the visitor..." – Marcel Proust

11,10 Your Maze

Go to the section on the Color Maze (page 106): make your maze and add it to your book.

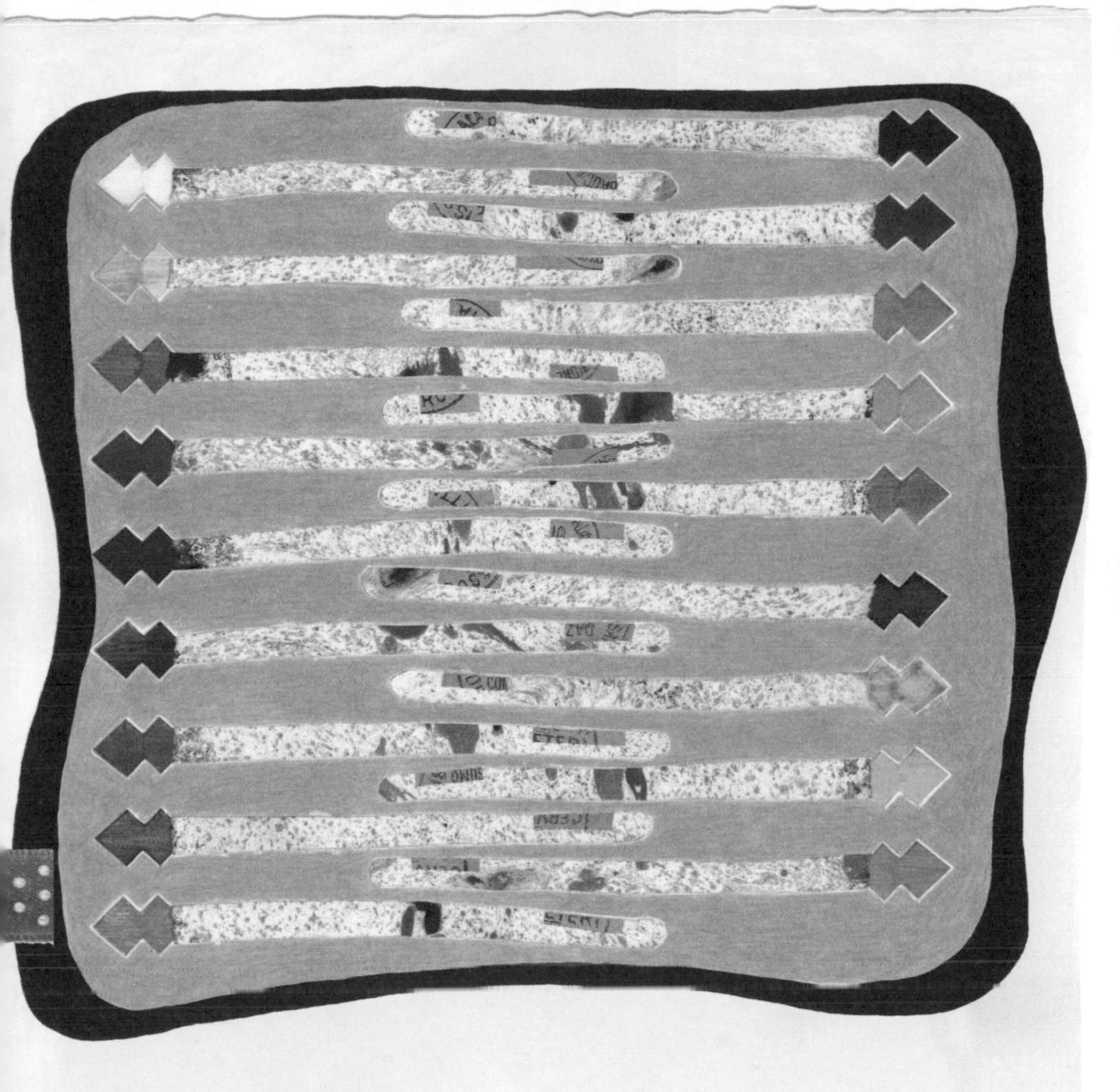

11.11 Color Box Portrait

Go to the section on the Portrait of Your Color Box (page 114): make your portrait and add it to your book.

11,12 Combinations

Go to the section on Harmony and Contrasts (page 122) and create transparent envelopes with colored bits. Take care while stapling it into your book... and write whatever occurs to you next to the envelopes.

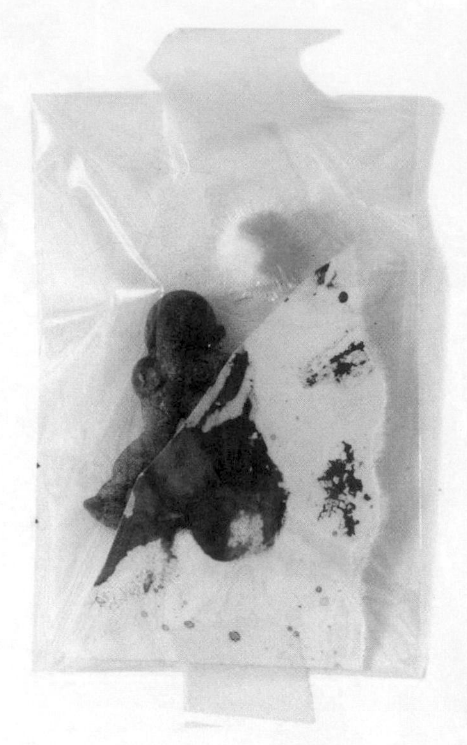

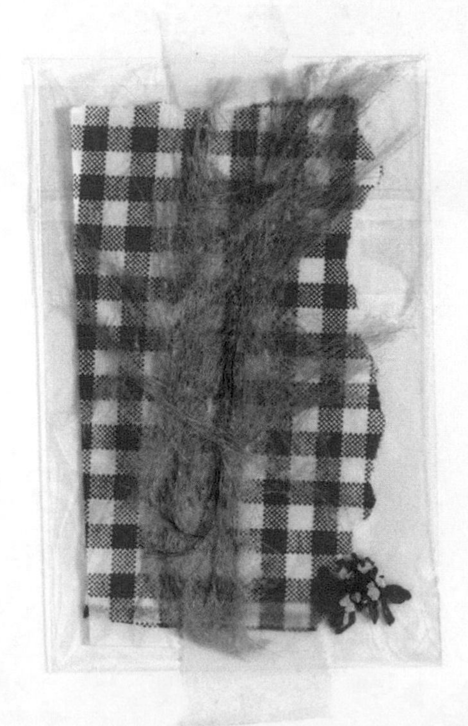

11.13 The End of The Color Dance

This is the end of the Color Dance I wanted to take you on, but hopefully, it's the beginning of the dance for you. I just want you to remember that color is both inside and outside you. It can be visible and clear, or transparent and hidden, needing to be discovered. You can feel it sometimes when you invent a color… a power that comes out of your hand, expressing something that you weren't even aware of! It's like standing in front of a crisp blue sky, feeling happy… we don't completely understand why, but we do too, in some way. We're always standing between light and shadow, some things are clear, and others hidden.

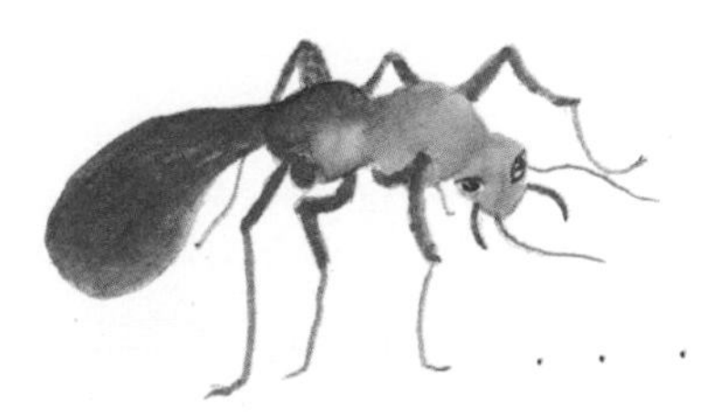

. . . keep looking!

I'd like to thank my children Nicola and Matilde, as well as my husband Giulio for their valuable contribution to this book. Cristina Nieto Gonzales freed me with her sensitivity. Thanks also to Manuel Nieto Gonzales, Chichita Calvino, Giovanna Calvino, Sophie Wolkieweiz, Christine Khondji, Benedetto Pietromarchi, Miguel Fabruccini, Darius Khondji, Azar Nafisi, Lisa Corti, Emanuela Benini, my father and my mother. Alice Hodgson for her grace and for sternly encouraging me to write. And thanks to Nathan, a 5 year old angel I met on a flight, as well as Violette. My thanks also to the innumerable people with whom I talked about color.

The Color Book

Translated from the original Italian by
Guido Lagomarsino & edited by Gita Wolf

For this edition:
Tara Publishing Ltd., UK <www.tarabooks.com/uk>
and
Tara Publishing, India <www.tarabooks.com>

Design: Nia Murphy
Production: C. Arumugam
Printed in China by Leo Paper Products Ltd.

ISBN: 978-93-83145-01-0